Trust is Ery Thing

JERZ TOSTON

Trust is Ery Thing

By: Jerz Toston

Cover Art Created by KREATIVEGRAFIKS.COM

Logo Designs by Andre M. Saunders/Jess Zimmerman

Editor: Anelda L. Attaway

Co-editor: Jerz Toston

© 2019 Jerz Toston

ISBN 978-1-7324523-9-8

Library of Congress Control Number: 2019918252

ACKNOWLEDGMENTS

First, I'd like to thank Allah (SWT) wit out Him this would not be possible.

Next, I would like to tell my kids Kaí, Meesh, Jerz, Deivyan, Riya, and Ceer this is all for y'all; never let anyone defer you or tell you that you can't do whatever you want.

My other half, BF, and soulmate Tambra aka Mrs. Toston 2 U thanks for always having my back no matter right or wrong.

Finally, my publisher Jazzy Kitty love ya.

Jus remember wit out loyalty there's no trust & Trust is Ery Thing!

DEDICATION

This book is dedicated to all my loyal fans because I appreciate their continued support and commitment to reading my books.

Ya Fav Author!

TABLE OF CONTENTS

TABLE OF CONTENTS

CHAPTER 1
Tired of Being Broke

"Sasha, Sasha wake up Baby, it's time to get ready for school."

This is tha way it went every morning. My mom would come wake me up while my dad made breakfast on tha stove. Once I was dressed I would go downstairs and eat my breakfast, then my dad would walk me to my bus stop.

But, this morning it felt different for some reason, my dad got down on his knees then said, "Sash Daddy loves you and I will alwayz be here for you no matter what. You do know that don't you?" I just shook my head yes as tears rolled down my eyes.

I understood exactly what he was say'n to me as my bus pulled to tha curb. I wiped my tears and told myself this will be tha last time I cried.

I had just gotten home from school when my dad said, "Hey Daddy's Girl, you want to go get some ice cream?"

I screamed, "Yes! Can we? Ooooh!"

While we were walk'n to tha store some guys walked up to us and asked my daddy if he could sell them some work. At tha time, I didn't know what he meant. My daddy said we didn't have any that's when he pulled out a gun and told my daddy to run his pockets. When my daddy refused, he put tha gun to his head. And all I remember was tha sound of that gun and something came fly'n out tha side of daddy's head. Then he fell face first, I screamed wit all my might then I sat next to my dad holding his bloody head cry'n my eyes out. It wasn't until tha ambulance came that I let him go. At tha moment, I vowed never to shed another tear again.

I was runnin late for school, as soon as I hit tha door I could see tha bus. I didn't run cause I knew my dog wasn't going to let old man Johnson pull off wit out me. When I finally got to tha bus, old man Johnson just stared at me.

"Damn Sasha, can you be on time one day."

Before I could say anything Layla said, "Boy, like you gon go to class anyway."

"I know that's right," he shot back wit a smile that would melt a snowman in a winter blizzard.

His name was Ahmad and he was a boxer but he was cool wit me and Layla so we would never cross that line. Me and Layla had all our classes together except one. At tha end of tha day, I was more than ready to go home, I met Layla at tha bus.

"What's up Sash?"

"Shit, I know I'm tired of catching this bus every day, we need a car."

"I feel you but we need money to buy a car."

"I know, aye Sash I was thinkin."

"Uh oh, here you go Bitch."

"Shut up and listen, I'm tired of being broke."

"So what are you gettin at?"

"We need to do a stick so we can get a few ones to get a pack."

"Nah Lay, I ain't try'n to sell no drugs plus, we ain't got no clientele."

"What Bitch, is you high? All we need is our moms."

"Girl you crazy."

"Nah, I'm serious, if my mom is going to get high I would rather her get it from me."

Now even though my mom got high, she was still beautiful. They say we could pass for sisters that's how much we looked alike; 5'6", caramel skin, long wavy hair, hazel eyes, and a nice ass like tha singer Beyoncé. While Sash and her mom were identical, 5'8", brown skin, short Fantasia style hair, brown eyes, and an ass like tha rapper Jackie O.

"Well, you sound like you got this shit all mapped out. So who we gon' stick and where we gon' get tha guns from?" I put her down wit tha whole plan.

"Bitch you crazy."

"Are you down or what, cause I'll do this Shit by myself if I have to."

"You my girl, you know I'm down."

"A'ight, we gon' make it happen Saturday."

"A'ight." We road in silence tha rest of tha way home.

Tha next two days flew by, I called Sash to make sure she was still down. She told me she was on her way up tha street to my house. When she got there she had on all black. I passed her tha 38 while I kept tha 40 for myself.

"Here take this mask." We waited until everybody was out of tha store before we went in.

As soon as tha clerk saw our weapons she said, "No shoot!"

"Where tha money at you Chink Bitch!"

"No lota money only this," she said passing me tha bills out of tha register.

We walked out of tha door, once outside we removed our mask and walked around tha corner. We went back to my house to count tha money.

"Fuck!" I yelled, "200 lousy Fucken dollars. I should go back and kill that bitch."

"Lay it's cool."

"Nah, it ain't cool, we could have gotton some serious time if we would have gotton caught and for what? 200 Fucken Dollars!" I picked up tha phone and dialed.

As soon as somebody answered I said, "Where's Drew?"

"Hold on, Drew come get this phone."

When he got to tha phone he said, "Who dis?"

"Ya cousin."

"Oh, what's up Layla?"

"I need to holla at you about something."

"Well, holla not on tha phone."

"Why is ya phone tapped?"

"Boy please."

"Well, go head then."

"Listen, I got 200 ones, what can you do for ya little cuz and don't try to beat me cause I got a scale," I said lying.

"Girl, I would never beat you if anything Imma give you more cause you my peeps. What do you want hard or soft?"

"Let me get it soft."

"A'ight, I'll be by in 30 minutes."

(CLICK) Tha line went dead.

"Lay, why didn't you get it hard cause we gon' cook our own shit."

"But we don't know how?"

"It's just like when we cook shit in Chemistry class, but instead of making tha bake bounce back it's goin to be coke." Within 30 minutes there was a knock on tha door.

"Who is it?"

"Girl, open this door."

"Sash, get that please." I opened tha door for him, Drew was 23 but only looked to be about 18.

"What's up Sash?"

"I can't call it Drew." He walked in tha kitchen where Lay was sett'n up shop.

"Cuz, you know what you doin?" I handed him tha doe and he handed me tha sandwich bag.

"That's a half ounce, I doubled up since y'all try'n to come up."

"So, how much bake should I put on this?"

"Well, it all depends on how good you want it."

"We want to beat out tha rest."

"Well, in that case, I would only put 7 on it. Where is your cell?"

"I don't have one."

"Here, you can have this one," he said handing me his burn out, "now, weigh out 7 grams of bake."

"I don't really have a scale."

"Sash look in my glove box and get that scale," he said giving me his keys.

When I came back Lay had tha powder in tha pot mashing it up wit a spoon that she had bent in a "L" shape. I weighed out 7 grams of bake and added that to it. Once it was evenly mixed, Lay had turned tha heat on low, put just enough water in tha pot, and worked her magic. After a few minutes, it looked like a cookie. She ran cold water on it as well as sitt'n it in a bowl of ice water which made it get super hard. I took a butter knife and went around tha edges then flipped tha pot over so tha cookie could fall on tha napkins that we had laid out on tha counter. Once it dried enough I put it on tha scale which read 19 grams. Shit, that was good we had an extra 5 grams, well, really 12. Next, we needed to get some bags, Drew said he was out and to just hit him when we needed more. But only next time, we would get what our money could afford which was fine by us. As he was leaving, my mom and Lay's mom were coming in. When they saw what we were doing they almost lost it.

"Here, let us know what this is hitt'n for," I said break'n them both off a piece which they gladly took and went into tha basement. Within minutes, they were back.

"Who cooked this up Drew?"

"No, I did," said Lay, "why Ms. Jean which is

Lay's mom said, "This is some real good Shit. I haven't had coke this good since Ms. Shirl cut her off."

"Girl, we ain't never had no shit this good."

"I know huh."

"Well, y'all won't have no problem sell'n this."

"Well, we gon set up shop at Ms. Cookies crib because we don't want no traffic here; not where we lay our head at."

"You just like ya dad." I had to smile at that statement.

For tha next few days, we got our hustle on, but when we were done we only had $350.00. And it went like that for tha next few months.

CHAPTER 2

Try'n to Get Our Money Right

It was tha last day of school and I was glad because now we could spend more time try'n to get our money right. It seemed like tha ride home took forever. One thing for sure, two things for certain, I'm gon put my license to use. I won't be on this bus for my senior year. As soon as we got off tha bus we went straight to Ms. Cookies. A few of tha guys were start'n to hate cause tha fiends didn't want their shit. Tha one boy Monk who was about 19 said that we had to find another place to hustle. Me and Sash had already made up our minds that we were not goin to be told where we could or could not hustle. So, we went and got tha two pistols we still had on lock from tha robbery.

"Sash."

"Yeah, Lay."

"I just want you to know that no matter what I'll alwayz have ya back and vice versa."

We both put our pinky up interlocked them then said, "Best friends and sisters for life."

Wit that being said, we tucked tha guns in our waistband and headed back to Ms. Cookies. As we reached tha steps to Ms. Cookies, Monk and his crews were walk'n towards us. Me and Sash remained calm.

As I reached for tha door, Monk yelled, "Hold up Shorty, let me holla at y'all!"

When he got close enough Sash spoke first, "What you want Monk? I'm not in tha mood for none of ya Bullshit today."

"Me either," I said wit an attitude.

"Listen, I done told you two Bitches that y'all had to find another place to get y'all money! This Shit around here is mines," then he looked at Lay and said, "unless you want to end up like ya old man, I would advise you to move on."

"Damn," I thought to myself, *"now why did he have to just say that."*

Lay said, "What did you just say?!"

"Bitch, you heard what I just said. Unless you want..."

Before he could get tha rest out Lay had pulled her pistol out, aimed right at his chest. So on cue, I pulled mines.

"Awe ain't that cute, now put them shits away for y'all get hurt."

"Listen here Monk, these niggaz around here might be scared of you but me and Lay ain't. So, just let us do us and it won't be a problem, capice."

"Nah Sash, I want, no I dare this Bitch Ass to repeat what he said about my daddy."

"Awe, is somebody about to cry? Put that gun down, you ain't gon use it. And as for ya daddy, I said if you don't want to end up..." That was all he got to say.

BONG, BONG, BONG, BONG, tha four shots at close range lifted him straight off his feet. Lay showed no remorse, so I walked over to his body, put tha gun in his mouth, and squeezed tha trigger causing his head to bounce up off tha pavement.

"Now, what was that you was say'n Nigga? This is a warning to anybody who tries to cross us. Don't let these pretty faces fool you! Any of y'all got something to say? If so, say it now!" But nobody said a word, they just turned and walked away.

For tha next few weeks, it was hot. I thought for sure, somebody would have dropped a dime on us but nobody did. In fact, a lot of people praised us for doing what they all wanted done but had no heart to do.

"Lay, this is not going to get it, we ain't gett'n nowhere."

"Sash, I was think'n tha same thing, we got to take a trip to tha city for ourselves."

"When we finish this we gon' see how much money we got and just go."

We finished tha pack two days later. We sat in Lay's kitchen and counted all tha money we had. We had a total of $8,100.

"Let's holla at Spikey." Spikey was an old head who took people up New York to cop.

"He said he would do it for two hundred and a ballgame but he wasn't going to be ready until tomorrow morning."

So we decided to grab another quarter off Drew to make an extra 300. We put it in bags instead of break'n off which was good because we have made damn near 800 off that quarter.

"Sash that's where we were going wrong. Shit from here on out, I'm only selling bags; we made damn near 800 off a quarter."

"I know, normally all we make is 350."

Tha next morning, Spikey was up and ready to go at 8 a.m. I gave him a buck before we left and let him know he would get tha rest when we got back. And since neither of us knew where we were going, we had to trust Spikey and hope that we wouldn't get beat because we were females. By tha time, we got to tha city it was a little after 10, Spikey stopped to use a pay phone. After about 10 minutes he came back to tha car I had to call poppi, he said he would meet wit us at his restaurant.

In 30 minutes, we arrived at his restaurant which was located in Spanish Harlem. We went in and were shown to a table in tha back. Within 5 minutes, a Black guy came to tha table.

Spikey got up and said, "Poppi how you doing?" wit his hand extended which he took.

Then replied, "Good My Friend, very good." He then introduced us.

Once tha introductions were over I said, "No disrespect Spikey but if you'll excuse us we got it from here."

A smile came across poppi's face then he said, "You heard tha lady, excuse yaself." Once he did I got straight to business.

"Listen poppi, I want to get one thing straight from tha door, we have no problem spend'n our money wit you..." Then Sash cut in.

"But we will not be taken advantage of and we do not expect any special treatment. So wit that being said, we have 8500 to spend."

"I sell bricks for 20,000; on tha breakdown that's 10,000 for a half and 5,000 for a quarter key so this is what I will do. I'll give you a half but tha next time you come you have to pay me an extra 2,000 on top of your order, 1500 for tha rest and 500 for me wait'n. Is that OK wit you ladies?" I looked at Sash who nodded in agreement.

"Yes, as long as tha work is good."

"Mama, I promise you will have tha best shit in ya town hands down. If I am wrong, you can come back and get your money but keep tha coke."

From that moment, I knew that poppi was a real nigga. We hit him wit tha doe and he told us where to pick up tha work. Poppi said he would see us in a few weeks and he also gave us his number then let us know to alwayz call a day in advance so that he could make sure he was around. Tha ride back was smooth but this would be tha first and last time we would ride wit Spikey. We will get a rental and follow him up and back. We just pay him more doe which was fine by him.

"Poppi was right, his work was far better than what we were gett'n from Lay's cousin Drew."

My mom and Lay's mom had both checked into rehab. They said they were tired of chasing that high; our prayers had finally been answered. We turned that 18 ounces into 24 and it was still top notch. All tha hustlers wanted to get their hands on our product so we decided to sell weight and dimes. We ended up making 26,000 off a that 24 but we did it in 4 days. I called poppi to let him know that we wanted to come up tha next day.

"You done already?"

"Yeah poppi, we don't hold them grams."

"Ok mami, I see you tomorrow same place."

We called Spikey to let him know to be ready in tha morning which he was definitely wit it. This time we got up there by 9 am since we left at 7 am to beat tha am traffic. Poppi walked in, we stood to greet him but he insisted we remain seated.

"Good morning poppi."

"Please call me José."

"Well, good morning José."

"And same to you Layla and you too Sasha." I handed him an envelope wit tha 2 stacks and another bag wit enough money for a bird.

"Listen, ladies I honestly didn't expect to see you for at least another week. This shows me that you are serious about gett'n this paper. So, what I'm going to do is front you another brick on top of tha one you brought."

"If I may asked, how much do we owe you?"

"Only 22,500."

"Ok, that's cool."

"I'll see you when you're done."

We went to tha same place to pick tha work up. We got home and went straight to work turn'n tha 72 into 96; dump' them for 9 a pop and still hitt'n tha block ourselves. Tha word had spread that we were indeed tha Bitches to see and in no time tha work was gone. We called José again to let him know that we were ready. He couldn't believe that we had dumped 2 birds in 6 days. Truth be told, we could have gotton rid of more had we had it. He told us we no longer had to come up there, he would have it brought to us because he was ready to really hit us. I let him know we wanted 3 and he said he was send'n another 5 on top of that and to hit him wit 110,000.

"Just call when y'all are ready."

It was a serious recession and we were tha only two Bitches as they call us wit work. A lot of niggaz let they pride get in tha way; they didn't want to buy no weight off two females that were only 16 at that.

Over tha next few months, we had New Jersey on lock. School was about to start back up and I was going to cop me something nice to go back in. Me and Sash were having a welcome home party for our mom at tha St. Patrick's Center wit only our relatives. They had been in rehab for 90 days; I hope that was long enough for them to stay clean after so many years of gett'n high. We arrived at rehab, we had to go in to sign them out. When they finally came out, I could tell they had picked up a few pounds that looked real good on them.

"Hey Mom," I gave her a big hug, "somebody has picked up some pounds.”

“Hey Ms. Jean.”

“Hey Sash, let’s get something to eat I’m starving.”

I turned up tha radio then pulled off heading to tha center. As soon as we pulled up I got excited seeing all tha cars.

“Why did we come here?”

“Oh, Mr. Rollins wanted to see you two,” I said lying.

As soon as we walked in everybody yelled, “Welcome Home!”

Tears started to roll down both their faces, my Nana Trish came over to give my mom and Ms. Shirl a hug.

“I’m glad to see you two ladies.” Sash’s Mom-Mom Patsy did tha same.

“I hope you two stay clean and leave those drugs alone; you’re to beautiful for that.”

Both our moms are what we call functional junkies. They got high but they also kept a job and made sure we were alright, that was a first priority for them. So now, it was our turn to take care of them.

“Mom, I was wondering, since school is in a few weeks if you could sign for a car for me.”

“What kind of car?”

“I don’t know, I was hoping we could go tomorrow.”

“We might as well go wit them,” Sash said to Ms. Shirl.

“Jean, do you hear these girls? They must have been hustling hard since we been gone.” I wanted to say, if you only knew.

We had a ball that night, I was glad to see our mothers enjoying themselves wit out being high. Afterward, Lay and I sat down to have a serious talk.

"Once we pay José we'll be up to almost 400,000."

"I know it's risky but I think we should spend it all."

"Hold off on tha cars til next week and just flip all that we have. What do you think?"

"Well, Lay all I have to say is that they say great minds think alike because I was think'n tha same shit." Just then my phone started to vibrate, when I saw tha caller ID I smiled. But what could he want at 1 am?

"Hello José, I was going to call you in tha morning, we need to see you."

"I need to see you also."

"Do you think you can come up in tha morning?"

"Sure, we'll be there by 8, no later than 8:30 a.m."

"OK, I'll see you then."

(CLICK) Tha line went dead.

"What did he say?"

"He needs to holla at us."

"I wonder what that's about?"

"Well, it could only be good."

"Yeah, you right."

"Well, I'm about to get a few hours of sleep. Before I forget, Ahmad called he said that he wanted to get down. Don't ask me how he found out but I did tell him that one of us would call him tomorrow."

"A'ight that's cool."

"Imma just crash on tha couch, I don't feel like walk'n home."

Tha next morning once we showered and dressed, we were on our way to see José. As usual we parked and walked into tha restaurant where José and another man were already having breakfast. They stood to greet us; José took this opportunity to introduce us to his older brother Sanchez. Once we were formally introduced we sat down.

"Would you ladies like something to eat?"

"Nah, we ate on tha way up here."

"Oh I see. Well, tha reason I asked you ladies here is simple, my big brother wanted to meet tha queens of Jersey himself. He did not believe me when I told him about you."

"Well, let me get to tha point ladies, José works for me so of course his prices will be higher than mines as he has to make his."

"And we totally understand that nor have we ever complained."

"Well, José has to go away for a little while and he likes you that's why he introduced you to me. So, from here out you'll be deal'n wit me; only thing that will change is tha price. I believe you are currently pay'n 20,000. Now, you will be pay'n 15,000." I couldn't help but smile.

Sanchez said, "Judging by ya smile that's a'ight wit you."

"Fo' sho," Sash said.

"Well, we came wit ya money José and 400,000 of our own money."

"Well, I'll give you 27 for that and throw you another..."

"I don't mean to cut you off but you don't have to throw us anything. We would rather just get what we pay for this time around and we say that wit no disrespect."

"No No mami, I totally respect and understand that. By tha time you return home your product will be wait'n on you." And sure enough, we got home to find it wait'n.

We had Camden, all tha way to Salem on smash; but this time, we were sell'n tha whole pie for 32,400. School started back in 5 days, now it was time to cop a car but we decided to go to this place in Delaware that my cousin Drew told us about called Fy'Heed's Used Cars. He said he would take us since he knew where it was at. I was impressed as soon as we pulled up on tha lot. I had no idea what kind of car I wanted but I wanted something nice; Sash knew what she wanted. As soon as we hit tha lot this money green Impala IT 08 wit peanut butter guts, they only wanted $17,500 for it that was a good deal. While she was inside doin tha paperwork I was still try'n to make my mind up between a 528I Wagon and X5. I ended up wit tha black on black Wagon for $16,600 and Drew told them to install this secret compartment that not even tha dogs could sniff out. I couldn't front, that shit was tha bomb. I was definitely goin to Rico's Rims & Radios to get tha works. Once we stopped at Rico's, we hit Dollar Tree to pick up some extra stuff we needed for school in a few days. Lay had some dubs on her Wagon since that was tha biggest she could get. I chose to go wit dueces, of course I had to spin thru tha city so niggaz could really hate. When I rode past streets, Bugsy and Slim I could see tha hate in Bugsy's eyes. He was one of them niggaz who let his pride stop him from copp'n from us. Tyreek on tha other hand was Bugsy's little brother who been try'n to get at me since Freshman year. I never gave him no rhythm. Now, don't get me wrong, he sexy as hell but he always lets his brother run tha show and that's a major turn off to me. I pulled up to tha light bumpin DaBaby's "Pop Star" which sounded good in my system. When Tyreek noticed it was me he motioned for me to pull over so I did just to make his brother mad.

When we got to tha car, first thing he said was, "My brother gon really hate now he was try'n to cop one of these."

I just smiled then said, "Is that right?"

"Yeah, when you gon stop act'n all crazy and let me take you out?"

"I told you when you stop lett'n ya brother run tha show."

"Why you try'n ta play me Sash?"

"I'm not try'n ta play you, I'm just keep' it real that's all."

"I feel you."

"Do you? Well, think about what I said, I'll see you around."

I pulled off slow just so Bugsy could get a look at tha car he wanted.

CHAPTER 3
Them Bitches Must Really Be Eat'n

"Yo Reek, you ain't Fuck Dat Bitch yet."

"Nah."

"Damn Nigga, what you wait'n for?"

"Why you up in my Shit Bug?"

"Nigga you beta watch ya mouth for I Fuck you up."

"Yeah what ever..." Before he could say anything else Layla pulled to tha light in this pretty ass Beamer Wagon on dubs bump'n Lil Baby's "Drip to Hard."

"Damn them Bitches must really be eat'n."

"I hear they got this shit on lock and dey bout dey work."

"Nigga stop pussy riden."

"Nah, I ain't doin that, I just give props where it's due."

"Well, I say Fuck them Bitches, I'll rob they ass. Let me catch 'em slipp'n, watch and see what happens."

Man, this nigga be bug'n all tha time. If he put his pride aside we could be eat'n too. Ain't nuffin wrong wit copp'n off no broads, I'm bout to do my own thing. Fuck him, brother or no brother and I'm definitely not going to let him rob my future wifey.

"Aye Bug let me ask you a question."

"What?"

"How come we don't just grab from Sash and Layla."

"Nigga I ain't copp'n off no Bitches!"

"Why not? Especially since they got tha best product in tha city and 9 outta 10. Tha niggaz we grabb'n from gett'n that shit from them but dey just putt'n all that bullshit on it."

"Nah, I'm cool, if you want to cop off them then do you but I'm straight."

"A'ight, then give me mines and Imma holla at Sash."

"Sell what you got and that's you."

"Nigga you lost ya mind if you think that all you gon give me is 1500 and truth be told, majority of this Shit is mines."

"I put all tha work in."

"You know what Bugsy, you right. Imma take this 1500 and blow like TNT." I didn't say another word, I sold my Shit then stepped off.

I couldn't believe it, off of 15 grand this nigga hit me wit 1500. I pulled out my phone, went to contacts found tha name I was look'n for and pushed send. After tha 3rd ring somebody picked up.

"Hello."

"Hey what's up Ma."

"Who this?"

"Damn, you didn't store me in?"

"Who this, Tyreek?"

"Yeah."

"Oh, what's up."

"I need to holla at you on some business."

"Shit, where you at?"

"On my way to my crib to grab tha rest of my doe."

"You a'ight, you sound like you upset."

"It's nuffin, can you swing thru or what?"

"Yeah, I'm on my way." (CLICK)

"Damn, him and Bugsy must have gotton into it."

I walked in tha front door greeted by my mom and little sister, I spoke and kept it movin. Once inside my bedroom I went to tha closet to get tha rest of my money out my safe. This was what I called my fall back doe and now was a time I needed to fall back on it. Even though it was only 11 grand, not including tha 1500 I knew I should be able to get something decent.

When my phone rang I smiled, "Yo, I'm out front."

By tha time I got outside, Bugsy and slim were comin up tha street. I didn't say shit, hopped in wit Sash and rode off.

"Damn ya brother had tha look of murder in his eyes."

"Fuck dat nigga, he tried to play me for tha last time."

"Look Sash, Imma get straight to tha point, I been wanted to do business wit you and Layla but my brother was on some I ain't copp'n off no females Bullshit. So, after I talked to you a little while ago I let him know that we needed to get at y'all but he still was on his Bullshit. It just don't make sense, tha nigga we holler'n at probably gett'n his shit from y'all going back to tha lab stretch'n it then sell'n that Bullshit to us. So, I told Bugsy to just give me my half and I was gonna do my own thing. This nigga try to play me. Nah, let me take that back, he did play me. He told me to finish what I had and that was me. I only had 1500 worth of work."

"Damn, so you need something for that; Imma hook you up."

"Nah, I had a little bit of doe stashed for something like this. I got twelve five all together."

"Ok Imma just give you tha half, you just owe me 3600. I'm not going to put no extra on it this time."

"I want it already done cause my cook game Fugazy."

"You don't know how to chef; Boy you better learn cause you could turn 18 into 24 wit no problem and still be oils. Now, for a stack I can show you."

"It's a bet." I took him to Ms. Cookies then called Layla and told her to bring me what I needed to Ms. Cookies.

"Tyreek on some real, you should have been did ya own thing. I know that's ya brother but you don't owe him Shit. Look how he did you and once you hit ya block wit this he gonna be mad cause he ain't gonna be able to sell his Shit. Then he gon want you to sell him Shit for tha low."

"Sash, I've considered all of this but truthfully Fuck 'em. My brother has held me back for too long, now I'm bout to do me and Fuck tha game up something serious." When Lay came I was ready to get to work.

"I see you finally decided to get on tha winning team. I just hope ya brother is a'ight wit it."

"Fuck that nigga, Layla he on some other shit that I ain't wit."

"I feel you and look at her, you couldn't wait for that."

"Now, you can finally go out wit him."

"Bitch shut up," I said throw'n a paper towel at her.

I took Tyreek through it step by step; I did tha first 4½ and he did tha rest. Tha first time he did it he only came out wit 5 but as I talked him thru it he got 6 on tha other 2.

When we were done I said, "Just add my stack to tha 3600."

"I was think'n I'll treat you to tha movies and dinner and we call it even."

"That sounds good to me," Lay said.

"Oh you must gon pay tha stack then."

"I can, it ain't bout nuffin," she said reach'n into her handbag; she must of thought I wasn't gonna take it.

"Well, are you ready Tyreek?"

"Yeah, but I'm goin to a different spot."

As soon as he walked out Lay said, "Damn Bitch, you gonna really keep my stack? You ain't Shit!"

"I know I've been told that a few times." We both started laugh'n.

"Nah, but here," I said handing her tha money back she'd just given me.

I got in tha car, opened tha stash spot, then told him to put that shit in here til we get to our destination.

"You know you still owe me huh."

"Nigga if you can huh, you can hear; I said you still owe me, I gave Lay her money back."

"I ain't got nuffin to do wit that."

"Boy please, I gave you a lesson in Chemistry 101; I wouldn't dare take my best friends money."

"A'ight, I got you, but can I still take you out tomorrow?"

"I'll think about it; make a right here then make a left at tha stop sign. It's tha second house from tha corner."

Before I got out I told her I would call her tomorrow wit her doe. She just smiled and pulled off. I'm gon' get her Sexy Ass, let me bust this Shit down so I can hit tha block for tha next few days. I pulled all-nighters; I didn't even call Sash for our date; I only called her to re-up. I didn't want to compete wit my brother so I set up shop in old man Smitty's house. I couldn't front I was kill'n 'em; I had made more money in 4 days than I did in 4 months hustling wit Bugsy. School was in 3 days; I had all my clothes and supplies. All I need is a squader until I made enough doe to get something nice. So I called my cousin to see if he was still selling his 97 Park Ave wit tha 22s. He let me know that some dude was supposed to buy it but he was bullshit'n around. So, I told him I wanted it.

"Do you think you can scoop me since I don't have no way to get to you?"

He told me to give him 30 minutes and he would be here. When I went outside to wait Bugsy and Slim pulled up in an old school 79' Impala wit 22s on it. I couldn't front, it was nice but I have not spoken to Bugsy since he played me last week. He got out and went into tha house. As soon as my cousin pulled up I jumped in his Caprice and he pulled off.

"Aye Slim, where did Reek go?"

"He got in tha car wit some dude."

"Oh a'ight, damn y'all still ain't talk'n?"

"Nah, I guess he still mad; he'll be a'ight in a few days," so I thought anyway, "aye Bug on some real, a few junkies said that Shit he got is tha truth. We need to get him to sell us some of that Shit; he got old man Smitty's house jump'n."

"Shit, them damn fiends said they only came around to cop off us cause Reek wasn't around."

"I'm try'n to tell you, we need to get some of dat."

"Nigga we alright, we up ain't we? So what you complaining about? We got this hot as whip and that nigga still on foot."

CHAPTER 4
We Suppose to Hook Up Tonight

"So how did ya date wit Tyreek go?"

"I don't know, we never had one. He been on his grind, we suppose to hook up tonight to do dinner and a movie."

"Did you call Sanchez?"

"Yeah, he said it will be here in tha morning."

"Can you believe this is our last year of school?"

"I know huh, I'm ready to walk that aisle to get that diploma."

"I heard dat. Well Sash, what are you doing for ya birthday next weekend?"

"I don't even know yet, I was think'n bout having a party at tha lagoon in Essington."

"Well if so, we need to start making flyers."

"We can call tha babe Angie now and see if she can have them by Sunday plus, we can post a few bulletins on Facebook."

"A'ight, let me hit Angie now."

"A'ight Imma call Tyreek."

"Make sure we still on." When I called he answered on tha 3rd ring.

"What up Sash? You keep call'n my phone and not say'n nothing."

"Damn I did, my fault. You know I got this iPhone so I probably touched tha screen by mistake. Are we still on for tonight?"

"Yeah."

"A'ight then I'll be by to scoop you at 8."

(CLICK) Tha line went dead.

"Girl you ain't Shit, you know that nigga did not call you."

"Yeah, I know that but he didn't, he said he would be to scoop me at 8."

"Umm Umm, he must of borrowed that pretty old school I seen his brother and slim in tha last few days," Angie said.

"If she get on it now she can have them by tomorrow."

"Shit, that's what's up, then we can give them out in school on Monday."

"I heard that."

We pulled up to my aunt Jazz's house and tha car was parked in tha driveway, this was actually my first time seeing it. It looked nice; it was cranberry wit white guts piped out in cranberry. It looked like it was a 2004, not a 97.

"I like this Cuz."

"Listen Reek, Imma be real wit you, only thing wrong wit it is it needs a oil change. I never took it because I ended up gett'n my Caprice."

"So, how much do you want for it Cuz?"

"I wanted 5 stacks wit ery thing but you fam, so just give me 4."

"Nah, Imma give you tha 5 stacks cause you already got tha works; rims, TV's, and system."

"I feel you and you can just keep it in my name until you want to get it switched over."

"A'ight, that's good look'n."

He signed tha title then slid me tha keys while I was pass'n him tha money we said. And it has automatic start then pushed tha button bringing it alive. When I got in, I knew that I wasn't going to be gett'n another car until tha end of tha school year. He didn't drive this too often, it only had

50,000 miles on it. I drove back to my house where Bugsy and Slim were out front cleaning their cars. Damn, who would have thought I would be out shining my brother. When I got out, Slim came over.

"Damn Reek, this you?"

"Yeah, I just grabbed it off my peeps."

"I like it."

My Brother just kept cleaning his whip but I saw him check'n my Shit out. I jumped in tha shower to get ready for my date wit tha lovely Sash. Once I was dressed I called to let her know I was on my way to scoop her.

Tyreek had just called to say he was on his way; I had just finished gett'n dress. My mom knocked on my door.

"Sash."

"Yes."

"Can I come in?"

"Yeah, come on in Mom."

"Wow, don't you look nice."

"Thank you, I'm going to dinner and tha movies wit a friend."

"I just wanted to let you know that next week I'll be going back to work at tha law firm so you won't have to foot all tha bills."

"It ain't about nuffin Mom."

"I know but still."

"Well, me and Lay thought that you and Ms. Jean deserved a break because no matter what tha two of you were doing, y'all always made sure we were straight."

"Well, finish gett'n ready and I'll see you later."

I grabbed my Gucci frames and handbag off tha dresser and made my way downstairs to wait for Tyreek. "She got me speedin in the fast lane, pedal to the floor mane, tryna get back to her love."

I opened tha door to see Tyreek pull'n up in this pretty cranberry Buick. I locked my door and got in.

"I see you went and got yaself a nice car."

"Yeah, it's no Beamer but it'll do."

"I like it, so where are we gett'n something to eat?"

"I'll let you decide that. Oh yeah, here you go," he said handing me an envelope.

"Oh, so is this ya way of tell'n me that I'm pay'n?"

"Nah, I invited you remember."

We ended up going to Hibachi's, after we were done eating we decided to see Saw V., that Shit was good as Shit, I would definitely recommend seeing it.

By tha time tha movie was over it was 11 p.m. We pulled up in front of my house and talked til 2 in tha morning, we had a lot in common. I also let him know that I was having a party next Saturday for my birthday at tha Lagoon.

"So, what do you get a girl who has ery thing for her birthday?"

"You can get me a nice card and I'll be happy. I'm not a picky person, it's always tha little things that mean so much. Well, let me get in tha house, I got a lot of stuff to do tomorrow."

I gave him a kiss on his cheek and exited tha car. That night I fell asleep wit Tyreek on my mind.

CHAPTER 5
Stop Pump'n My Shit

I pulled up in front of Old Man Smitty's, Slim was posted up out front.

"What up Reek?"

"Nah, what's up wit you?"

"Shit, just try'n to get a few ones."

"Not right here you ain't, take that Shit back around tha corner." Phil came walk'n around Tyreek.

"Yo Tyreek, what's pop'n? Reek that thing you got now is Bullshit, it ain't nuffin like that Shit you had tha other day."

"What you talk'n bout Phil."

"Ya boy right here been pump'n ya Shit ."

I looked at Slim, "Yo Nigga, what tha Fuck is up wit you?" A few more fiends walked up say'n tha same Shit.

"Look Imma hit y'all off but don't nobody sell my Shit but me or Old Man Smitty."

"Hold up for a second," I used my key to let myself in, "what up Reek?"

"Yo, you know that nigga Slim out front pump'n tell'n them he got my work that's why it's been a little slow."

"Don't worry about it."

I walked back outside wit tha fiends off. Slim had slid off while I was in tha house but I knew where to find him. So, I went back in to get my glock then I walked around tha corner and sure enough he was lean'n on tha green box talk'n to Bugsy. I walked over didn't say Shit, I pulled my pistol out and smacked Slim in tha face wit it. Before I could hit him again Bugsy grabbed me.

"Hold on little brother what's tha problem?"

"Tha problem is that ya man posted up in front of my spot sell'n Bullshit but tell'n tha fiends it's my work. Now tell me what part of tha game is that. He lucky I didn't just pop his Fuck'n top."

I had to calm Reek down cause he was a loose cannon.

"I told Slim not to do that Shit but I guess he did it anyway."

"Don't get it wrong, if you out there and they gon' buy ya Shit so be it but don't tell them ya got my work cause I'm tha Fuck'n one who had to reimburse them." Slim just stood there wit blood comin from tha side of his head.

I pointed my pistol at him then said, "Next time my brother will be walk'n around wit ya face on his shirt, I promise you that," then I looked at Bugsy, "you my blood so don't cross that line." Then I walked off.

"I don't know why you went around there after I told you not to."

"Cause that's where all tha money at. If we had some better work we could be eat'n a whole lot more than we are now."

"Nigga we cool, we don't want for Shit...do we? A'ight then."

"Man Fuck that, I'm bout to do my own thing."

"If that's what you want to do then do you. Just don't come runnin to me when Shit gets Fucked up or niggaz be on ya heels."

"Awe Nigga Fuck you, you always taken Shit to tha heart. I'm wit you, Bullshit coke and all," I said laugh'n.

"You wasn't laugh'n a minute ago when Reek smacked ya ass wit dat glock now, was you," then I started laugh'n.

"Nah, if he wasn't ya brother..." Bugsy interrupted.

"If he wasn't my brother what?"

"I would pop his top."

"Bugs you keep try'n that tough Shit. I see you ain't say nuffin when he told you not to cross that line. I don't play no games-you know that, brother or no brother. If he gets outta line my moms will have one son left."

CHAPTER 6

Tomorrow tha First Day of School

We had rode around tha whole city given out flyers, we even went to Salem and Brick City. I told Sash I was going in early tonight so that I could be rested for tha first day of school tomorrow. She let me know that she was doin tha same.

As soon as I came in tha house I could smell Turkey chops, fried potatoes, corn, and biscuits. I went straight to tha bathroom to wash my hands and prepare for dinner. My mom yelled up to say dinner would be ready in 5 minutes, so I decided to get my clothes out for school. I didn't know what to pick out, so I just went wit my sky blue and peach Fendi dress wit tha match'n shoes, something basic.

"Lay dinner is ready!"

"I'm coming down now Mom." We sat down to eat.

"Well, you ready for your last year of school?"

"Yeah, I can't wait to walk that aisle to get that paper."

"Baby I'm so proud of you, after all you have been through you never gave up."

"Mom you were my reason to keep striving to not give up."

"I knew that you would eventually get it together, I'm proud of you."

After we finished eat'n I helped wit tha dishes then headed upstairs to take a shower and switch my clothes for tomorrow. After about 30 minutes, I ended up going wit my pink and white DKNY sweat suit wit a white shirt that said DKNY in pink and my white on white Air Ones. I had to make sure ery thing was in order for school tomorrow. I put my frames and necklace on tha dresser then laid down to get some sleep.

I had just gotton out of tha shower and I was tired as hell but I still had to get my clothes out for school. I went into my closet and came out wit my black Gucci sweat suit, red Gucci Tee, and my black Gucci sneakers. I turned off tha light, as soon as I got in tha bed my phone rang, I picked it up.

"Hello."

"Hey Sexy you busy?"

"Nah, I was busy gett'n ready for bed that's it."

"Oh My Bag, I was just try'n to score."

"You don't have enough to hold you down til tomorrow?"

"Yeah, but I was gett'n low but I can wait. Do you think you can get wit me before school? I just want to make sure my peeps will be straight."

"Oh I feel you. Yeah, I'll just call you around 6 or 6:30 a.m. when I get up."

"A'ight Imma let you get some sleep; I'll just get wit you in tha AM so sleep tight and dream about me."

"Boy sit down, I got a lot of better things to do than to dream about you."

"Damn Sash, you sure know how to hurt a niggaz feelings."

"Well, I'm sorry I didn't know you was so...what's tha word I look'n for, sensitive."

"Yeah that's it, only when it comes to you. Sash don't act like you don't know how much I like you. Shit, I only been try'n holla since our Freshman year."

"Tyreek, I would have hollered at you if it wasn't for ya brother."

"I know, I know. Well, you ain't got to worry about him I don't Fuck wit him like that no more." I quickly filled her in about tha Shit wit Slim.

"Damn, that's some crazy Shit."

"I know Bugsy told him to do that Shit cause that Dumb Ass Nigga do whatever he tell 'em to do. Well, go ahead and get ya beauty rest and I'll holla in tha morning."

"What was you try'n to do anyway so I'll know what street we on?"

"I'll be on 33rd Street."

"A'ight, I got you."

"No doubt, good night my future wifey."

"Boy you crazy, bye." (CLICK)

Damn this nigga got me blush'n all crazy even though he's probably right. I could see myself mess'n wit Tyreek especially since he don't deal wit his brother and Clown Ass Slim no more. I had to admit, he got his paper up fast and we was a lot like me. Didn't want no handouts, wanted ery thing from tha muscle. I closed my eyes and fell asleep only to be waken up by my alarm clock.

"Shit!" I said out loud.

It seemed like I just went to sleep. I hit tha snooze button and dozed back off only to be woken up again by my mom.

"Sash get up, you don't want to be late ya first day." As soon as she walked out my phone rang.

"Hello," I said wit an obvious attitude.

"I don't care nuffin bout that, get ya ass up!"

"I'm up I'm up."

"A'ight, I'll see you in tha parking lot."

"I was gonna ride wit you but I got to get at a few people before I go."

"Oh Shit! Damn I almost forgot, I got to holla at Reek too Shit!"

"A'ight, well I'll see you there."

"OK." I hung tha phone up then went into tha bathroom to get ready.

"Tyreek, Tyreek!"

"Yeah Mom."

"It's time to get up and get ready for school."

"I'm up Mom."

"OK, I'm going to make breakfast so get dress Baby." loved my mom to death there's nothing I wouldn't do for her.

Once I was out tha shower I went into my closet to find something to wear. When I came out I had my red and white Sean John sweatshirt, white Tee, and white on white ones. My mom said it was chilly outside so I figured I would be cool wit my sweat suit on. I grabbed my chain wit tha iced out "T" and my Sean John stunners. By tha time I got downstairs I had to put my food in tha microwave. As soon as I started to eat Sash called.

"Good morning Sexy."

"Good morning to you too, I'm about 5 minutes away, be out front."

"A'ight," I said wit a mouth full of food. (CLICK)

"Boy slow down before you choke."

I ran back upstairs to get my book bag and tha money. I gave my mom a kiss and headed out tha door to be met by Sash pull'n up. I told her to follow me, I drove around to Old Man Smitty's. I got in and handed her tha bag of money. Then she gave me my shit and said I don't have to count this, do I.

I looked at her and said, "One thing for sure, two things for certain you can trust me always. Remember Sash, Trust is Ery Thing." When I was gett'n out she said something that shocked me.

"I'll see you in school future husband." Then she pulled off wit out giving me tha chance to respond.

I went into Smitty's put tha work up and made my way to school.

When I pulled up Lay was already there talk'n to a few people and Ahmad; I parked right next to her.

"Damn, I see you Sash," Ahmad said referring to my car, he had been gone all summer visiting his family in Saudi Arabia.

I just smiled and replied, "It ain't nuffin major."

"Many Men Wish Death Upon Me. Blood in My Eyes Now I Can't See. I Put a Hole in a Nigga for Fuck'n wit Me."

Tha loud music caused everybody to turn around to see who was bump'n like dat. When I saw tha car all I could do was smile. Lay asked who that in that nice ass car. Before I could respond Reek was pull'n in next to my car.

"Oh, no wonder you was all smiles." As soon as Reek got out Shonda and her crew walked over.

"Hey Tyreek, you look'n good as usual in that Sean John sweat suit."

"That's what's up."

"So I know it's tha first day of school but if you need a date for tha prom let me know."

"I already have a date."

Me and Lay just looked at one another; neither of us could stand Shonda she was always so extra. I loved tha look she had on her face when Reek said he had a date already.

"Well, if you don't mind me ask'n, who you taken?"

"Sash," he said grabb'n me by tha waist.

"What!" she screamed. I even was surprised but I didn't pull away.

Lay spoke and said, "You heard him and yes they are a couple," she added.

She looked at me and had tha nerve to say, "I see you lowered ya standards."

I went to grab her but Reek pulled me back then responded wit, "Nah, I actually lowered them when I dated you last year." We all busted out laugh'n at that.

"See that's why I dumped you."

"Nah, you must have forgotten, I stop deal'n wit ya nut ass." She just huffed and stormed off.

When she was outta ear shot I pulled away then said, "Why did you say that to that broad?" Then I turned to Lay, "and why did you tell her that we were a couple?"

"Well ain't y'all?" I gave her a look that said Bitch why you try'n to put me on tha spot.

"Well?" Reek said.

"Well what Nigga, are we a couple?"

"Oh nah, we just friends. Oh that's what's up," he said walk'n away.

"Bitch is you stupid or just retarded?"

"Neither, damn can't a bitch play hard to get?"

"Shit, you been doin that for tha last 3 years. I know you better not let him get away."

"He been after me too long to give up, especially when I'm giving him a little rhythm."

"A'ight, don't let it bite you in tha ass."

"Come on let's look at our schedules and get to class before we be late."

We got to tha office and asked for our schedules. Ms. Shilow handed us our schedules. This year we had every class together even Homeroom. As soon as we walked in tha bell rang. Lay sat in tha last seat leaving me to sit in tha seat next to Reek. I turned to look at her, she was smiling ear to ear.

"Let me find out you stalk'n me."

"Boy sit down, I don't know if you noticed or not but I am a smartass," I said punching him in tha arm.

"Excuse me Ms.," tha teacher said pointing at me.

"Sasha," I said.

He looked at his book then said, "Ms. Williams, please keep your hands to yaself." He was about to say something else when tha bell rang.

"What's ya next class?"

He looked at his schedule and said, "Some Bullshit."

"Come on Sash lets go, we have to walk to tha other end of tha build'n."

"We can walk and talk I'm going that way, I got Home Etc."

Lay said, "So do we, is this fate or destiny?"

"Girl you alwayz talk'n crazy."

"Reek let me see tha rest of ya classes," Lay said, "damn, yeah it's definitely destiny; you in 4 outta 5 classes wit us."

Tha rest of tha day flew by, we gave out a lot of flyers and posted a few around tha school. By tha end of tha day, I was ready. My phone had been blow'n up all day, I let everybody know I was in school and would get wit them at 2 o'clock. When we got to tha parking lot, everybody was stand'n around check'n to see who was driving what car. Lay told me she would see me at Ms. Cookies, she had to holla at a few of her folks.

She jumped in, turned tha ignition, all you heard over everybody else was "All Eyes on Me, I Live tha Life of a Drug Dealer til tha Day I Die." I could see tha hate in Shonda's face.

Reek pulled up, got out his car and said, "Later if you ain't to busy..."

"I ain't never too busy for you."

I could see Shonda look'n so to be petty I put my arms around his neck and gave him a peck on his lips then hopped in my Beamer. I turned up tha volume since she was still watch'n.

"She got me speedin in the fast lane pedal to the floor man, trying to get back to her love..." and I pulled out real slow.

Yeah, I'm definitely gon' wife her soon. I need to formally ask her to tha prom, I'll do it this weekend at her party. I pulled out my phone and dialed.

"Hello."

"What's up Lay."

"Nuffin."

"I need to ask you a question."

"Go head."

"What does Sash want for her birthday? I was think'n bout a nice Tennis bracelet wit her name on it."

"Yeah, that will work."

"OK thanks Lay."

"No doubt."

"Aye Reek..."

"What's good Ma?"

"You really like Sash huh."

"Yeah for about 4 years now. I would say I'm wear'n her down now."

"Boy you crazy as shit but between us, she feel'n you. If it wasn't for ya brother you would have been had a shot."

"A'ight Reek, Imma holla at you and don't tell Sash I told you that cause she will be mad at me."

"Don't worry, I won't tell her." (CLICK)

Let me shoot over to Philly to see if I can get this piece made by Saturday. I had a hard time finding a parking spot, I ended up parking in tha garage. I walked over to Market Street Gold.

As soon as I walked into tha store Tony said, "Tyreek My Man, long time no see."

"What it be like Tony?"

"You tha Man."

"I need something but I need it by Saturday."

"What you need?"

"I need a Tennis bracelet wit tha name "SASH" on it."

"Oh you got a lady friend; must be special for you to spend...how much you try'n ta spend?"

I went in my pockets and pulled out what I had on me.

After I counted it I said, "2600."

"For another 1500 I can have a necklace to match."

"A'ight, I want it ICY."

"Well, just give me an even 5,000 and it will make her neck and wrist cold all year around, I assure you."

"That's a bet."

I gave him tha 2600 and rolled out.

CHAPTER 7

Not Stop'n My Money

"Bugsy, what we gon' do? Ya brother stop'n all tha money. If we keep doin it like this we gon' be eat'n at tha mission."

"I was think'n tha same thing Slim so that only leaves us one option." I looked him in tha face to make sure we were on tha same page.

"You sure that what you want to do? That is your brother."

"Fuck that Shit! Brother or no brother, if a nigga stop'n my money than Imma do what I gotta do. We gon' do it Saturday cause I know he gon be at that party. And believe it or not, so will we after we hit Old Man Smitty's."

"Did you say Saturday?"

"Yeah why?"

"Nah that's perfect, Old Man Smitty is leaving town Friday and won't be back until Sunday."

"How you know?"

"My aunt is going wit 'em."

"Damn, they still Fuck'n around?"

"Yeah, she ain't goin nowhere, especially since ya brother got him up right now."

"You know we ain't gon' be able to sell that Shit around here."

"Don't worry about it, my Maryland nigga called me today said he try'n ta come holla Sunday. So hopefully, he got enough to fill his order."

"I don't think we gon' get too much paper; he keep that Shit at my moms so we can't even go in there."

It's cool, we gon' get a nice piece outta Old Man Smitty's."

"Say no more, it's on Saturday."

CHAPTER 8
Car Shop'n

I couldn't believe how fast tha week went by it was Friday already and we had one more period left. My phone was vibrating so I took it out to see who it was.

"Damn Sanchez," I put my hand in tha air.

As soon as she called on me I asked if I could be excused to tha bathroom. She pointed to tha pass on her desk; I grabbed it and hurried to tha bathroom.

"Hello."

"Hey, I know you're in school but something has come up and I have to leave town for 2 weeks."

"Is ery thing a'ight?" I asked.

"It's nothing I can't handle. I just wanted to make sure you and Sash were a'ight and to apologize for having to miss her birthday party."

"Actually, we do need to holla, we're going to add another 13 to our order to make it 40."

"A'ight. Plus, I'm going to put an extra 2 in for Sash; I'll give her a call Saturday to say, 'Happy Birthday'."

Over tha past few months we had grown to love Sanchez like a big brother because it wasn't alwayz about business. When he called he often called to check up on us; that let us know he cared and it was more than just a business relationship wit us. I walked back into tha class, just as I was putt'n tha hall pass back tha bell rang.

"Hey Sash, that was Sanchez he said to tell you he was sorry that he was gonna miss ya party but something came up and he was leaving town for 2 weeks. I put our order in for 40 and he said that tha extra 2 are for tha birthday girl.”

“Are you serious?”

“As a heart attack.”

“Wow, he’s giving me 72,000 for my birthday.”

Since tha recession we raised tha price to a stack and that was a steal compared to what everybody else was charging.

“You know what I’m going to do?”

“What you gon’ do Sash?”

“Upgrade like Beyoncé.”

“Shit I’m going to tha lot as soon as I go to tha crib to pick my mom up.”

“What you gon’ do wit ya car?”

“Shit, my mom alwayz got it, anyway, give it to her.”

I was glad to see that my mom was already home when Lay dropped me off.

“I’ll see you later,” she said as I was gett’n out.

“Imma hit ya phone when I get back from car shop’n.” I walked in tha door greeted by my mom.

“Where you on ya way to?” I asked.

“Well, I figured it was time for me to get my own car so I was going to look around.”

“I got a better idea, since you love my car so much why don’t you just keep it?”

“I can’t do that.”

“Well, I plan to get me another car today thanks to Sanchez,” she had a look that said what are you talk'n bout, "he gave me 72,000 for my birthday so let's go car shop'n."

I ended up wit tha new Caddy truck that I immediately dropped off at Rocco's to have tha works done. Start'n wit a pair of 28-inch Caselli's, a 17-inch flip down in tha back, a 10 inch in dash touch screen flip out, two 8-inch TV's in tha head rest, just for show three 15-inch Rockford Folgate subs wit a 3500-watt match'n amp and highs, to top it off that were pushed by 2400 watts of tha same brand equipped wit tha PS3. Rocco said he wanted to do it himself and could I pick it up in tha AM which was cool.

"Don't forget my automatic start."

"I got you Sash, just relax and I'll see you at 10' o'clock tomorrow morning."

By tha time we stopped to get something to eat it was 9 o'clock. When we made it home I went straight to Ms. Cookies, Lay was already there, I tried to look upset.

"Damn, you must didn't see anything you liked judging by tha look on ya face."

"Nah, I just grabbed me a red on white truck."

"Oh, you wanna look down on everybody when you riding by. Is it out front?" she asked opening tha door.

"I can't pick it up til tha morning."

"Oh, you got something fresh off tha show room floor."

"Nah, I wouldn't say that."

"Don't get me wrong it's nice."

"Then why don't you seem happy or excited about it."

"I don't know."

"Well, let's get to work cause we got a long day ahead of us tomorrow."

"I know, that brought out tha smile I've been try'n ta hide."

"I knew that would make you smile; I still have to go up to Philly to pick my dress up."

"I knew you would wait til tha last minute so I picked it up when I got mines."

We both got TOI from TOI East to make us some hot Gucci dresses; I couldn't wait til tomorrow.

CHAPTER 9
Tha Funeral Brought Sanchez Back Home

"Hello mami."

"Hello papi."

"Hello Sanchez, how have you been?"

"I have been fine."

"So, how is José deal'n wit tha circumstances?"

"He's fine, he'll be home in 18 months."

"I'm sorry that it took something like this to bring me back home."

"When is tha funeral?"

"Tha day after tomorrow."

I talked to my parents for a few hours then I made my way to my uncle Hector's house. My uncle was a very powerful man here in Cuba, he was tha reason we had tha states in a headlock wit tha cocaine. I was gett'n them for 10 and dump'n them for 15 but that would soon change. After this visit tha prices would definitely drop like Dow Jones.

I pulled up to my uncle's house and waited to be buzzed in. Once tha gates started to open, I made my way up tha hill to tha front of tha house which sat on acres of land. I got out tha car to be greeted by two bodyguards who wasted no time at all patting me down then escorted me into tha foyer where my uncle and 3 friends were play'n a game of Dominoes.

"Uncle Hector," I said upon entering tha room, everybody looked up.

"Sanchez!" he screamed leaping up from tha table wit his arms stretched out.

While we embraced he said, "Your mother said that you would not be in until tomorrow."

"I know but there were a change in plans."

"It doesn't matter you're here now and how is Juan doing?"

"He's fine, he'll be home in 18 months."

"Sorry to hear about Nana Louis."

"Sanchez, no need to feel sorry she was 92, she lived her life."

"Sí (Yes), I suppose you're right."

He continued to talk while having a seat to finish his game. Once tha game was over he excused himself so that we could talk privately.

"What seems to be on ya mind Unc?"

"I am having a problem wit an old friend of mines José Carbone; he seems to have forgotten who is in control around here. Not to mention, he's undermining my operation on a daily basis; that's why I haven't been able to send you a lot of product."

"I was wondering what was going on wit that."

"Well Unc, there's only one thing to do about that," I looked him in his eyes so that he could see tha seriousness in my eyes before I said, "kill him if he was tha reason behind my Shit coming up short! Then he and anybody else who got in tha way had to die."

After he filled me in on all tha details I let him know that it was a done deal and since he was very well guarded I had something in mind for him but I needed to plan it out for a day.

I had just gotten dressed when my cell started to ring, I couldn't help but smile when I looked at tha Caller ID.

"Tony what's good?"

"Tyreek your pieces are done and they are as you would say, fire."

"I'm on my way as we speak."

First, I stopped at South Street to grab something to wear but couldn't find nuffin so I decided to just go to King of Prussia after I hollered at Tony. When I saw tha necklace and bracelet I was impressed to say tha least.

"Damn Tony, you did tha damn thing on these babies."

"So you think she will like it?"

"Fo' sho, Shit all this ice, who wouldn't. I need a new bracelet for myself."

"I got just tha thing for you." He went into tha back and returned wit a bracelet, watch, and earrings all that match.

"Well, what's tha damage?" I asked.

"For you Tyreek 2,000, anybody else 3500."

"I got 1800."

"Got Damn, I'm giving you a playa deal 2 grand."

"It's me Tony."

"And only because of that will I give it to you for that."

He put it all in boxes and I was on my way to King of Prussia to pick up some hot Gucci Shit. By tha time I got to King of Prussia I just wanted to get in and get out. I went straight to Nieman Marcus and grabbed me a pair of blue denim Gucci jeans wit an all-white Gucci button up wit tha red and green down tha sleeves and on tha pocket and tha white Gucci sneaks to match tha shirt. There was no need to go any further, I already had a pair of Gucci frames so I made my way to my car. It was 6 o'clock when I got back to Jersey, I called Sash to see where she was at. It was obvious she was upset probably because I hadn't called all day to say Happy Birthday.

"Where you at? I need to holla at you for a sec."

"I'm home talk'n to my mom and Lay's mom."

"Is it cool if I swing by?"

"That's up to you."

"A'ight, give me 10 minutes."

I can't believe he didn't even say Happy Birthday not to mention he hasn't called all day." Lay walked in while I was Bitch'n.

"What's wrong now Sash?"

"She's tripp'n cause that boyfriend of hers just now call'n and he didn't even say happy birthday."

"And he's not my boyfriend."

"Well then, you really shouldn't be upset." I heard Reek pull'n up, I tried to hurry to tha door.

"Sasha Williams." I turned to face my mom.

"Yes."

"Have a seat, we want to meet this Reek guy." Lay opened tha door and told him to come in.

"Shit, I was hoping she came out but Fuck it, Imma have to meet my future mom-in-law one day. I wonder whose truck this is; that shit is fire."

I turned my car off and grabbed tha bag off tha seat. When I got to tha door, Lay was push'n it open for me.

"What up Lay?" I said walk'n in, "hello Ladies, how is everybody doin tonight?"

"Just fine."

"Lay and Sash I did not know y'all had older sisters," I said making them smile.

"Well, I see you have good taste," Ms. Shirl said, "so you are tha one who has my daughter so happy lately."

"Mom!"

"Mom what? I'm not going to embarrass you."

"Sorry I didn't call all day but I been runnin crazy try'n to get right for tha big party tonight, Happy Birthday," I said hand'n her tha bag.

"Well, did you find what you wanted?"

"Yeah, I got some fly Gucci Shit. Oh I'm sorry, please excuse my mouth."

"Well, looks like we won't be tha only ones in Gucci," Lay said.

"Oh y'all wear'n Gucci? Guess I better find something else to put on."

"Boy if you don't rock that Shit! Opps my bag," Lay said.

"I don't know what has gotten into these kids now days, I remember a time..."

"Oh God Girl, you better hush ya mouth."

"As I was say'n, oh never mind."

"Are you gon' look at ya gift or not?" Reek asked.

"Yeah," Lay said, "cause you know we all want to see what is in tha bag." I pulled a long red box outta tha bag, when I opened it I was speechless.

Everybody said, "Well, are you gon' let us see or not?"

I was stuck so Lay said, "Let us see," and walked over taking tha box out my hand.

I just walked over to Reek and gave him a big kiss, not even caring that my mom, Ms. Jean or Lay were in tha room.

I could hear my mom say, "Oh, you must really like my daughter to spend this kind of money."

"Well to be honest, I've been after ya daughter for uh...4 years. So, I would say I really like her,"

I had to look at that necklace and bracelet again, "it was going to say Sash but I figured might as well add tha 'A'."

"It wouldn't have mattered to me."

Lay looked at both of us and asked, "Does this make it official?"

I looked at Reek and said, "Well, you have to answer that, not me."

"You know what I'm gon' say."

"Well, I'm gon' say YES."

"Well it's bout time," he said wit a smile.

"Let me go get dressed; Reek you might as well ride wit us. I know you seen Sash's new truck outside."

"Damn Sash, you try'n make it hard on a nigga coming like dat tha new Caddy truck on 28s. A'ight, I'll be back in about 2 hours."

As soon as he left I said, "Damn, he really likes me."

"Nah Sash, dat nigga in love. He said he was gon' get a tennis bracelet, not all this," she said point'n to my ice, "I need me a man."

"Y'all need to start gett'n ready."

It was tha day of Nana Louis funeral, I had ery thing set up just perfect. I would attend most of tha funeral then slip out so that I could rid my uncle and myself of Mr. Carbone since he was in tha way. I calmly slipped out without anybody noticing, I made my way across tha street and into tha abandon building onto tha rooftop. I put tha gun together and looked through tha scope, Mr. Carabello will never know what hit him.

After about 15 minutes, people started to come out. As soon as I seen my target I squeezed tha trigger and it was over. One shot thru tha heart, all that was heard where tha screams of tha onlookers. I made my way off tha roof and back to tha church without anyone noticing. I gave my uncle a wink to let him know tha job was done.

Later that evening, we talked business and he let me know that he would be charging me only 5,000 a brick which was lovely even though I would still be leaving my numbers tha same except for Layla and Sasha. They would only pay 10,000.

"Oh Shit!" I picked up my phone and punched in a few numbers.

"Hello." I started singing "Happy Birthday" when I was finished Sash thanked me for her new truck.

"What truck? I didn't..." I had to stop in mid-sentence, "you're welcome."

She must have sold those 2 birds and copped a truck. We talked for a few minutes then I let her know that I would be back in 2 days and that I had some good news for them when I came back.

"Sash enjoy yourself tonight and I'll see you in 2 days." (CLICK)

Lay walked in look'n real fly wit her black Gucci dress and match'n stiletto's and frames; she had on her diamond necklace wit tha earrings and watch to match.

"You look'n real fly Sis."

"And you tha same." I had on tha same dress but white wit white Gucci shoes, my jewelry that Reek got me set it off.

It was 9 o'clock when Reek pulled up, our moms had left already to make sure tha food was in place. When Reek got out his car my mouth dropped, he had tha same thing I had on, well same color. Of course Lay had to say something.

"Y'all are too much alike, I swear!"

"Damn, you want me to change."

"Nah, for what? It looks good on you and so does yours."

"Awe ain't that cute, let me get a picture of y'all."

Once we were done wit our Kodak moment we were out. When Sash put on that old cool C "Glamorous Life" her shit was stupid loud and it was nowhere near even halfway up.

"Sash you definitely makin a nigga step his game up." When we pulled up it was J Peed and Tha line was long.

"Damn, it ain't nowhere to park."

"Why ain't it?" I said pull'n into tha spot that said, **'RESERVED FOR BIRTHDAY GIRL'**.

All eyes were definitely on us when we pulled up in my husky truck. We stepped out look'n like sure superstars, we made our way to tha front of tha line. Tha bouncer started to say something until Ms. Jean came to tha door and let him know it was my party. We walked into tha sounds of "How you feel hater's ya hatin' didn't work. Thanks to y'all I'm tha hottest thing on Earth…" Plies had everybody partying, it was packed. I can see now that a lot of people are not going to get in and it was only 10 o'clock; I was having a ball.

"Aye Sash let's take a few flicks wit those two ladies over there," she said point'n to our moms.

"Come on," I said. Reek was already at tha picture booth flick'n it up.

"Make sure you got ya mask pulled over ya face."

We hit tha door like tha police. We ram shacked tha whole crib coming up wit 54 ounces and $40,000. I was a'ight wit that, once we had ery thing put up we made our way to tha party.

"Damn Slim, them bitches got this Shit jump'n like a motherfucker."

"I know, look at this line."

"Oh Shit!"

"What's up?"

"We ain't wait'n in this line, that's my cousin at tha door, come on," and sure enough, we got straight in, "I knew you was good for something Nigga."

"Awe go head wit that Bullshit."

"Yo, there go Reek, come on."

When we got over to him I said, "What's tha deal Little Brother?" He looked at me and said what's up and kept it movin.

"That nigga know he can hold on to some shit. He'll be call'n later to borrow some money to get back and Imma tell 'em I ain't got it."

"Aye Bugsy I can't front, them two broads are sharp as shit," I said point'n to Layla and Sash.

"Look at them two clowns staring." I turned around to see who Sash was talk'n bout.

"Damn, I hope they can see us as hard as they look'n."

Tha DJ put on T-Pain's *"Buy You a Drink,"* I grabbed Reek and we hit tha dance floor. I was impressed, he could dance his ass off; he was wit me step for step.

"What you smile'n for?"

"Nuffin, I just can't believe after 4 long years I finally got you."

"Like you said, you wore me down." When tha song switched, we moved to tha side.

"Reek."

"What up Ma?"

"Thank you for this necklace and bracelet."

"Anything for you Sash, anything. You hear me? Anything!"

"Stop, you making me blush; let's take a picture." We got to tha booth, my brother and Slim were there flick'n it up.

"Aye Reek, take a picture wit us."

"Nah, I'm cool."

"Baby go head, don't act like that; he is still ya blood."

I went over to join them, we took 2 flicks. One wit tha 3 of us and one wit me and Bugsy. Then Bugsy told Sash to come on.

She said, "Nah, y'all go head."

"Yo Little Brother we gon' have to get along; on tha real, if that's ya girl."

I just looked then said, "Listen Bugsy, that Shit you did was Fucked up and I can't just forget that Shit! So until I do, I'm not Fuck'n wit you! No disrespect intended."

"None taken." And he walked off wit a smile on his face.

Me and Sash took a few flicks then her mom came over to take a few wit us; followed by Lay and her moms.

At tha end of tha night I was tired as shit, I was going straight home to bed. Sash pulled up in front of her house after dropp'n Lay off down tha street.

"Would you like to come in?" I looked at my watch it was 5 after 2.

"Yeah, I guess I can come in for a few minutes."

We sat on tha couch and talked til we both fell asleep. I awoke to my phone vibrating like crazy.

"What up Smitty? You blow'n my shit up all crazy."

"I just came home and my front door was wide open."

"Are you try'n to tell me?"

"I'm not try'n to tell you, I am tell'n you somebody robbed us."

"Fuck!" I yelled causing Sash to jump up, "I'm on my way!" (CLICK)

"What's wrong?"

"Somebody broke into Old Man Smitty's so I'm bout to go see what they got."

"Damn." I could tell by tha look on his face that they probably took what ever he had.

So I told him, "Reek if you need me for anything I'm here for you, anything. You hear me?" He just nodded and walked out tha door.

When I got to Old Man Smitty's tha door was Fucked up and so was tha house. I went to tha spot where tha coke and money was and of course it was gone.

"FUCK! FUCK! FUCK!" I yelled, "I swear when I find out and I will find out who did this, there will be Hell to pay! Smitty you better not have anything to do wit this Shit! So Help Me God!!!"

"Reek, I would never do no Shit like this; not tha way you be look'n out. Plus, I wasn't even in town." Shit he was right but he could have set it up.

"Call somebody to fix this door and I'm going to get an alarm put in and cameras; I'll be back."

I went to my moms house to make sure ery thing was in order. I went straight to my safe, tha $60,000 I had in there was still there but I was still out $40,000 and a brick and a half; somebody would have to sell that Shit. My phone started to vibrate, I never looked at tha caller ID.

"What!" I yelled into tha receiver.

"Damn, excuse me for call'n to see if you were Ok."

(CLICK) Sash had hung up before I got tha chance to respond so I called back.

"What!" she said when she picked up.

"I'm sorry, I didn't look at tha phone I just picked up."

"Well, is ery thing ok?"

"Nah, niggaz hit me for 54 ounces and $40,000."

"Shit, do you have a clue who it was?"

"Not at all."

"Do you need me to hit you and you can just hit me back when you get straight?"

"Nah, I'm cool."

"You sure?"

"Yeah, but I do want to spend $60,000 wit you."

"A'ight but you gon' have to wait, I got to go holla at my peeps. He just called and said he was in town and wanted to have breakfast wit me and Lay."

"Oh a'ight, just hit me when you done; I got a few things to handle."

"Reek."

"Yes Sash."

"Please be safe."

"No doubt." (CLICK)

Lay got into tha truck and then immediately sensed something was wrong.

"You a'ight Sis."

"Not really." I told her what had went down wit Reek.

"Sash, I bet you that it was Bugsy and Slim.

"You think so?"

"Why else would they come to our party and he can't stand us?"

"I know huh, I'm not going to say shit though, he'll figure it out. We just got to be careful and don't get caught slip'n." We pulled up to tha restaurant to find Sanchez already in his car wait'n.

"So, I see you brought ya self a nice truck."

"Yeah," I said givin him a hug.

We went in and found a table, once we ordered and our food arrived we got to business.

"I have great news that I'm sure you will enjoy. Tha same as I did, my uncle has kindly dropped tha price for me. So, I shall do tha same for you and only you. Everybody else will still pay 15 but you will now pay 10 a piece."

All I could do was smile and say, "I love you Sanchez."

"And I you," he replied wit his own smile.

"You have made my day papi," Lay said smile'n. We finished our breakfast and headed our separate ways.

"Sash, do you believe this $10,000 a bird? I'm gonna keep our numbers tha same too. Sash, Sash...”

“Huh?”

“Did you just hear anything I said?”

“Nah Lay, my mind was somewhere else. What did you say?”

“I’m not charging my numbers.”

“Me either but I am going to let Reek get them for tha same thing we get them for.”

“Do you, I respect that. So, do you think he is going to take work from you on tha front?”

“Nah I already asked, he said he was just gon’ spend his last 60 grand to get back.”

“Damn he was hold’n, so 6 bricks will definitely get him back in tha game.”

“I’m going to Ms. Cookies.”

“Me too.”

We pulled up and Lay got out, I told Lay I would be right in. I called Reek and told him to come thru so I could holla at him face to face. He said to give him 15 minutes and he would be thru. So, I sat in my truck and waited listening to Raheem Davue’s customer; I was so into it that I didn’t see Reek at tha window. I motioned for him to go around and get in on tha driver side.

“Damn, this is my Shit!”

He said, “What you know about this?” And started singing.

I had no idea that he could sing like that. Wow was all I could say when tha song went off.

“Oh, I sing a little bit.”

"A little...Boy sit down. You know you can sing."

"I heard that."

"But on a serious note, I just talked to my peeps and he lowered tha price so I decided to let you get them for tha same as me and you only..." he quickly interrupted.

"Well, how much is that gon' be?"

"Is 10 good enough for you?"

"10 what! Nigga stop play'n...well, then let me get 6 right now."

"Hold on, they won't be here til tomorrow morning; I'll just add ya 6 wit our order. Can you hold off til then?"

"Shit for that number I can hold off til next week. Imma start pump'n weight to my cousins in Maryland for 20 a bird. On my next flip, I got a few young boys Imma put on," he grabbed my face, kissed me then said, "that's why I love you. I know it's hard to believe but I've been in love wit you for 4 years. Now I know it's gon' take you a minute for ya feelings to catch up but I'm a patient person as you know."

"Honestly Reek, I can't explain it but I love you too." Wit that he tongued me down.

Lay yelled, "A room for that Shit you 2 love birds!"

CHAPTER 10
Ready to Get in tha Game

That night of tha party Ahmad had surprised me by tell'n me he was ready to get in tha game but he wasn't willing to play tha corner. I asked him how he expected to get his doe up if he wasn't going to hit tha block. Ahmad quickly let me know that he had peeps who wanted weight and that he would get it from his uncle. But since his uncle was now facing some serious time for attempted murder he didn't know where else to go. Then he remembered we were on tha come up.

"Well, what are you try'n ta do?" I asked.

"How about I just call you when they call me."

"Why don't I just give you a few and you hit me wit tha doe."

"He said that because we are in a recession, that he charges 28 sometimes 29 a brick. We been in recession for about 5 months now and doesn't look like it's going to be over any time soon."

"Well, I'll give you 3 for 21 apiece."

"Ok, meet me at tha Super Fresh in 30 minutes." I pulled up and Ahmad came walk'n over to my car.

"Here's 33 I should have ta rest tomorrow."

"No problem, I'll see you at school."

"Do you want me to bring it to school?

"Nah, I'll holla at you after school about that."

"Aye Ahmad."

"What up Lay."

"Be safe and keep ya eyes and ears open at all times."

"No doubt, good look'n Lay."

"It ain't bout nuffin Ahmad, we have to look out for each other."

"I feel you on that." Wit that said I pulled off headed to holla at my sweety in Delaware.

I still had no clue who broke into Old Man Smitty's House and robbed me. It has been 3 weeks, whoever had done it sure wasn't sell'n any of that coke but it would never happen again. Not only did we get a steel door that even tha police would have a hard time kick'n down but we got an alarm and cameras that tha average person would think were just porch lights. And to top it off, I brought 2 top of tha line pitbulls; a boy and a girl both 6 months and already killers. I named them Black and Fire because tha boy was all black and tha female Fire because that's what color she was. I only had them for 3 weeks and they were trained to go if I or Smitty gave tha command. They were free to roam about tha house all day and night; if they had to use tha bathroom they would let you know. If I wasn't in school they were wit me; they did not like anything or anybody except for Sash. I don't know why, they just did.

School was gett'n ready to let out for tha day so I had to figure a way to get these roses to Sash. When it hit me I sent Lay a text ask'n her if she could unlock Sash's truck so I could put tha roses in there. She texted me back and said to go ahead, by tha time I get there it would be unlocked and sure enough it was. Just as I put them in and locked tha door tha bell rang. I jumped in my whip and pulled off slowly waving to Sash and Lay as they came out of tha building.

When I got to my truck there were a dozen white roses on tha driver seat and a card that read:

"JUST WHEN YOU THOUGHT THAT NO ONE CARED OR THA WORLD WAS AGAINST YOU ALONG COMES THIS ONE PERSON WHO BRIGHTENS YOUR DAY WIT A SIMPLE CARD THAT SAYS I LOVE YOU"

And it was signed, Ya Number One Fan Tyreek. I looked over at Lay who was smile'n from ear to ear.

"Awe he is just so damn sweet, kind of reminds me of my sweetie Sikaí."

"Well, when am I going to meet tha guy who has you going to Delaware 4 or 5 days a week?"

"Soon Sash soon, I promise. I just met his mom and dad; they cool as shit; especially his dad."

"He lives wit them?"

"He lives wit his mom."

"Oh, they not together?"

"Nah, but they mad cool."

"Does he hustle?"

"Nah his dad does, He just spoiled. From what I hear and can see, his dad has Wilmington in a chokehold. I need to ask Sanchez about him."

"Why do you say that?"

"Oh cause, one time when he stopped by to hit Kaí wit some paper I could have sworn he answered his phone and said what up Chez but then he walked off."

"Bitch you crazy, I'll find out." Matter fact, she pulled out her phone and dialed.

"Hey Big Bro, I need to ask you something."

"What up Sis?"

"Do you by any chance deal wit a guy in Delaware by tha name Jerz?"

"Why, is he giving you problems?"

"No no, not at all."

"Good cause I like him, I would hate to have to kill 'em."

"Nah I'm dating his son. I thought one day when you called him he said Chcz but I wasn't sure."

"Yeah, he my man."

"Is he gett'n paper?"

"Yeah, probably triple what y'all gett'n."

"Oh well excuse me."

"Nah Sis, I wasn't say'n it like that."

"I know, I'm just play'n...well, that's all I wanted."

"Ok love ya."

"And I you." (CLICK)

"Now who crazy? He said that Kaí's dad is his peeps and he gett'n crazy doe, I mean crazy doe."

"Well, that will explain why he don't hustle; he ain't got to. Shit if my pops was still alive I would not be hustling but he not so like Rick Ross said "Here I Am.""

"I feel you, my pops called me tha other day talk'n all stupid. I kindly let him know that when he chose to walk out and not keep his promises was tha day he stop existing to me and I hung up on his ass! Lay I was 5 years old when he left; that nigga has called me 4 times in 12 years. Now what kind of love is that!" I said gett'n pissed off so I changed tha subject, "so you really feel'n Kaí huh?"

"Yeah, he's a keeper."

"That's what's up, as long as you happy. I would hate to pop his top for Fuck'n wit my sis."

"I heard that. Aye you want to shoot down there wit me?" We were interrupted by my phone.

"Hello...Oh hey Kaí."

"Nuffin...Yeah, I'm gon' come see you; me and my sister come'n thru...Nah, she locked in already, I'll hit ya phone when I get close."

(CLICK)

"Damn, how you know I wanted to go?"

"What else you got to do?"

"Well let me stop by my house to grab a couple ones so I can go to Bottom of tha Sea and get me one of those good platters."

"How you know about Bottom of the Sea?"

"You know my cousin Prishay lives down there."

"Oh yeah, I forgot."

"Matter fact, let me call her and see where she at I haven't seen her in a while." I called her phone.

When she picked up she said, "Damn Cuz I thought you forgot my number."

So I shot back, "So you don't know mines or are your fingers broke?" She started laugh'n.

"So what's up?"

"Nuffin was headed that way and was call'n to see if you were around."

"Yeah, I'm in tha crib on Facebook, I actually just sent you a comment."

"Well, I'll be down within tha next 30 minutes."

"Make sure you stop by."

"You know I am." (CLICK)

"So I guess that means you will be drop'n me off."

"Y'all can come if y'all want." When I pulled up in front of Kaí's house there was this nice ass cream on cream S600 sitt'n on dub dueces.

"That's Kaí's dad car."

"Shit I likc that."

"Yeah, that's tha new one." As I was dial'n his number he and his dad were walk'n out of tha door; I closed my phone then got out.

"Hey Kaí, hey Mr..." He cut me off in mid-sentence.

"What I tell you bout that Mr. Shit? You try'n ta make me feel old?"

"You are old Dad."

"I can out do any young boy; you better just hope you look this good when you reach my age. Didn't you hear Jay-Z 30s is tha New 20s?"

"Yeah, but did you hear Lyfe Jennings 30s Ain't tha new 20s It's tha Same Old 30s?"

"You got that one but you just remember what I told you."

"I know but you know how my mom be trip'n."

"I know, I told you come stay wit me for a while. I'm sure she'll appreciate you when you're gone."

"A'ight, I'm hit ya phone. Oh yeah, don't forget to pay my bill."

"You ain't got no doe?"

"Nah, I spent it on tha new Jordan's."

"Well here take this nickel (500), pay ya bill and treat ya girl to dinner."

"We just friends Dad."

"Oh my fault, you better change that for somebody else scoops her little pretty ass up."

I started blush'n, all I could say was, "I like ya car."

"Thanks, I love that truck.

"Oh, I can't take credit for that it's my sisters," I said pointing towards Sash. Sash rolled down tha window and waved then rolled it back up.

"I see good looks run in tha blood; I would love to meet ya mom if she doesn't have a man."

"Nah, but she needs one."

"Is she good look'n?"

"I'll let you be tha judge of that," she said pull'n out her iPhone to show me a picture.

Once I got to tha one I wanted I turned my phone around to show him.

"Got Damn! This ya mom Shorty?"

"Yeah."

"She bad as Shit! If you don't mind me ask'n, how old is she?"

"35"

"We bout tha same age. Well, take a flick of me and when you go home tonight let her know that I would love to take her to dinner if she don't mind. You can call Sikai and get my number."

"Hold still so I can take ya picture."

"Ok wait, let me make sure you got a good one."

"A'ight that's cool." I started laugh'n when all 3 of his phones started ring' at tha same time.

"Hello, hold on…Yo hold on…What's up? Yeah, give me 40 minutes."

(CLICK)

"Yo Oh Ok, I'm on my way." (CLICK)

"What's tha deal? Nah he cool, he right here. Nah, that's ya Shit, you gotta give him room to breathe."

"You right, he can stay wit me."

"Yo save that Shit! How about I get him his own spot then."

"What? My son don't got to sell no drugs. As long as I'm alive and free he gon' be a'ight and even if I'm not, he got a hefty trust fund set up. I'll holla at you." (CLICK)

She gon' call right..."

Before he could get tha last word out you heard, "My Baby Mama Give Me Drama on a Daily."

"What up? Nah, I was done talk'n...can you borrow what? I ain't got no money. How much? A'ight, I'll leave it wit Sakai." (CLICK)

"Yo when ya mom come give her this," he said reach' into his pocket pull'n out a $50 bill, "just tell her that you had to...never mind cause you'll never get it."

"Well a'ight, I'll holla at you later."

"Why ya sister didn't get out?"

"She probably on tha phone."

"Oh well, you make sure you show ya mom that picture."

"Imma show her, don't worry I got you." He jumped in his Benz and pulled off bump'n that Meek Mill's "Flamers."

"Ya dad is cool as a fan."

"Yeah, I know."

"Is he really gonna get you ya own spot?"

"If my mom don't stop trip'n he'll do it just to piss her off."

"I thought she was cool?"

"Yeah, she is at times but she always want Shit her way and don't know how to take NO for an answer."

Layla rolled down tha window, "I'll be back, I'm gett'n ready to hollar at Prishay."

"You talk'n bout Bombshells daughter?"

"Yeah why?"

"Nah she like my peepz, her mom mess wit or use to mess wit my moms best friend."

Oh I heard that. Y'all a'ight or y'all try'n to roll?"

"You still going to Bottom of the Sea?"

"Yeah."

"Well I'm going."

"Me too, I could go for a number 21."

"Don't you got to wait for ya mom."

"Shit, I almost forgot that fast. Oh nah…I'm good, here she comes."

Before she could park I handed her tha doe and let her know I would be back. She said hi to Sash and Lay and then pulled off.

"Now we can roll." When I got into tha truck I formally introduced Kaí and Sash.

"Nice to finally meet tha guy that my sister keeps break'n her neck to see."

"Sash!"

"What? That's how I feel when you do that Shit wit me and Reek."

"Not to be in y'all business but are you talk'n bout Tyreek Anderson from Camden?"

"Yeah, how you know Reek?"

"It's a small world, that's my 1st cousin."

"Boy stop play'n."

"I ain't play'n, watch this," he pulled out his phone, dialed a number then put it on speaker, "what up Little Cuz?"

"Shit, what's good wit you."

"Nuffin, was just sitt'n here wit Sasha."

"Wit who Nigga?"

"You heard me, Sasha."

"Nigga how you know my wifey?"

"Because he mess wit Layla," Sash quickly responded.

"What!" he yelled, "so she been going to Wilmington to see my cuz?"

"Yup."

"Talk about a small Fuck'n world. Where y'all at?"

"We in Delaware Nigga," said Kaí.

"Damn, we gon' have to get together this weekend."

"What, you forgot I was coming up there this weekend."

"Damn, I sure did."

"Where's Bitch Ass Bugsy?"

"I told you we ain't Fuck'n wit one another."

"You got tired of let'n his Bitch Ass run tha show?"

"Fuck you Kaí."

"I been told you bust his ass; you see he stopped that Shit wit me after that time I kicked his ass."

"Where Uncle Jerz?"

"He just left."

"Did Sash meet him?"

"Yeah her and Lay?"

"Why he want to holla at Lay mom?"

"Cause she showed him a picture."

"Awe Shit! Well, I'll see you Friday. How you gett'n up here?"

"Probably my dad, he said he wanted to see Aunt Rose anyway."

"A'ight and don't be try'n to hook my baby up."

"Come on Nigga, since I know that's wifey Imma watch her like tha police on a stake out. And if a nigga try to holla Imma check his ass from tha door."

"Well, I'll get at you in a few days." (CLICK)

"Tha world is just too damn small. Shit, I might have to move up Jersey if you play ya cards right."

"Nah Nigga, if you play ya cards right."

We pulled up on this side street over Westside, Prishay was on tha porch talk'n to a few of her friends. I pulled in front and got out.

"Hey Little Cousin," I said giving her a hug, "where Aunt Shonny?"

"In tha house." Lay and Kaí got out.

"Hey Prishay," they both said.

"What you doing wit my cousins Kaí?"

"Oh this my peeps," he said point'n to Lay.

"Well Damn Sash that's how you doin it?"

"We do it when we do it." We walked in.

"Hey Aunt Shonny!" me and Lay yelled.

"Hey what y'all doing down here?"

"Well, Lay came to see Kaí so I tagged along so I could see Prishay."

"Oh I see, you only came to see Prishay."

"No I came to see my aunty too."

"Kaí you not speak'n?"

"I spoke when I first came in."

"Ya mom just left." I heard a loud system pull up then tha front door opened.

"Hey Uncle Jerz," Prishay said giving Kaí's dad a hug.

"Damn, y'all way over here?"

"This my aunt's house."

"Bombshell ya aunt?"

"Yup," Lay said.

"Hold up Prishay, you just said Uncle Jerz."

"He ain't my real uncle but I love him like one."

"Bombshell, I was stop'n by to give you this," he said hand'n her a bag of weed.

"Is this Soul Diesle?"

"You know that's all I blow," he started to walk out then turned to Prishay, "did ya dad give you tha money for ya sneaks yet?"

"No."

"Well here," he went in his pocket and came out wit five 20's, "is that enough?"

"Yeah."

Bombshell said, "That's more than enough."

"I don't know cause this nigga sneaks be like 150 or 175; his shit cost more than mines."

"Did ya mom come?"

"You know she did."

"A'ight I'll holla. Aye Jerz you going to $2.00 Tuesday tonight at tha Good Shot Bar?"

"Probably, why?"

"If you do, swing by and scoop me."

"A'ight I got you." And he was out tha door.

"I know I'm hungry," Lay said.

"Well, let's go to Bottom of tha Sea."

"Shay you wanna ride."

"Yeah, let me get a ride in that pretty truck you got outside."

"That was a birthday present from my big brother."

"Well Damn, I hope my dad hit me off like that for my birthday in 2 months."

"Kaí you don't even got ya license."

"I'll have them in 3 or 4 weeks, I'm in Drivers ED now."

Aunt Shonny said, "Let me see this truck," she went to tha door then said, " well Damn, you do a lot better than a whole lot of so-called ballers, I'm feel'n that."

"Mom, I'll be back."

"Ok."

It was after 9 o'clock when we made it back home. I wasted no time show'n my mom tha picture of Kaí's dad.

All she said was, "Who is that sexy man?"

"Somebody who would like to get to know you if you are interested." She gave me a funny look.

"Come on Mom, it's my boyfriend's dad. I was in Delaware today at his house and his dad was there so I introduced him to Sash and he said that he would love to see tha woman who produced such beautiful children. That's when I showed him a pic of you which of course blew him totally away ask'n if you had a man which I kindly said no but you could use one."

"Damn Lay, you made me sound desperate."

"Mom you are! When was tha last time you had a man or even got ya self some?"

"Layla Jackson!"

"What? I'm just keep'n it real."

I had to think, *"Damn she is right, I have not had a man since her father was killed and as far as sex goes it's probably been just as long. Now don't get it twisted I do please myself often but that's about it."*

"Mom, Mom."

"Huh?"

"Look at you try'n ta remember. Would you like me to get his number so you can call him tonight because he said if you were interested in dinner for me to call Sikaí and get tha number."

"Let me see that picture again...well I guess." I couldn't dial tha number fast enough.

"Yo."

"Hey Sexy, what is ya dads number?"

"Damn, let me find out ya mom wants a piece of my pop."

"Boy shut up and give me tha Damn number; get ya phone Mom."

"Ok what is it?"

"302-275-1414"

"Ok, I'll call you when I get out tha shower." (CLICK)

"Well, now tha rest is up to you."

"What's his name?"

"Jerz, call him."

"I will."

"A'ight, I'm gett'n ready to get in tha shower so make sure you call him Mom."

"I will Layla."

As soon as I heard tha water I flipped my phone open and went thru my contacts until I came across what I was look'n for them. I pushed send after tha 4th ring I hung up only to have my phone ring a minute later. I let it ring twice before pick'n up.

"Hello, somebody just called my phone?"

"Is this Jerz?"

"Yeah, who dis?"

"This is Jean."

"Who Jean?"

"Layla's mother, I was told that you wanted me to call."

"Oh tha Sexy Lady from tha picture Lay showed me?"

"I wouldn't say all that but yeah that's me."

"I did tell her to tell you to call but only if you were interested in going to dinner."

"Oh I see, well she left that part out."

I lied; I didn't want to seem too desperate. We talked gett'n to know one another, he let me know off tha back that he was a hustler which I didn't have a problem. I didn't know if I should tell him about my past now or wait until I went to dinner wit him. I decided to tell him now, after I did I also let him know I would understand if he had second thoughts.

"Listen Jean, tha past is exactly what it is tha past."

"If you did get high all those years like you say and still look that damn good. I know from being in this game so long that you were what I call a control addict so I'm not at all having second thoughts."

I came downstairs to hear my mom tell'n him that she use to get high. I knew she would eventually tell him but not from jump. Whatever he said in response must of been good cause he had my mom cheeze'n like a teenager wit a crush. After what seemed like forever she finally hung up tha phone look'n at me.

She said, "He seems like a nice guy."

"So when are y'all goin to officially meet?"

"He said that he would be up this way Friday to drop Sikaí off at his sister's house."

"Did he tell you who his nephew was?"

"No and I didn't ask?"

"Well, Reek is his nephew."

"Wow, talk about a small world."

"I know, me and Sash said tha same Shit I mean thing."

"Well, let me get ready for work tomorrow," she said heading up tha steps humming a Keith Sweat song.

CHAPTER 11
Still No Word

It had been almost 3 months and still no word on who ran in Old Man Smitty's.

"Black, Fire," sit I said as I walked to tha corner to make sure there were no more dogs in tha park.

It was clear, so I whistled and they came runnin full speed. While they were runnin around tha young boy Spit came up to me.

"What up Reek?"

"Shit what up Spit."

"Nuffin just try'n ta get this paper right."

"I definitely feel you on that."

"Aye Reek."

"What up Lil Homey?"

"Let me ask you a question if I may."

"Sure shoot."

"How much do you charge for a onion (ounce)?"

"I charge a stack."

"Is tha work good?"

"Come on Young'n I got tha best Shit."

"I don't know I be copp'n off ya brother and Slim and I know that Shit is trash."

"Right."

"Nah, actually it's fire but they want 1500 an onion. Now I know we in a recession but Damn."

"Aye Spit, by any chance is that Shit T-shirt white?" He went into his pocket and pulled out an 8-ball.

"Yeah see." I didn't want to jump to any conclusions so I asked him how long they been pump'n this.

"About a week because for real for real; they normally got booked up garbage but my cousin told me they had some drop. So I been gett'n at 'em for tha past week."

"Well here's my cell number, just holla at me when you ready."

"A'ight, I'll be call'n in a little bit."

"That's cool." Then he stepped off.

"Black, Fire lets go."

When they got to me I put their leashes on; I knew I would find out eventually I just needed to be sure first. Tha only other people who had this drop other than me were Layla and Sasha and I know they didn't sell these niggaz no work. Everybody else was put'n too much on it so I know Slim and Bugsy had to be tha ones. I pulled out my phone and called Sash but all she did was confirm what I already knew. She also told me that her and Lay thought it was them but didn't say nothing cause they didn't want to be in tha middle. I respected that and now it was all make'n since; him and Slim at tha party that night, my blood began to boil.

My phone started to ring, "Hello."

"What's up Cuz?"

"I can't call it; I know I was suppose to been get wit you but Bugsy had come through for me but now he keep talk'n bout he wait'n."

"So what's good?"

"Do you think you can get ya hands on some of that T-shirt White Shit he had a few months back?"

"Yeah, that's all I sell."

"How much for a bird 38?"

"Nah, 36 stacks for you and it's drop fo' sho. Do you want soft or hard? Ya best bet is soft cause you can put 320 grams of bake and turn 36 into 48 and still have tha best in Maryland."

"Shit you ain't got to tell me twice; let me get that Johnson and Johnson then."

"A'ight, aye Wayne was it around September when you got that from Bugsy?"

"Yeah why?"

"I was just curious."

Now I knew it was them my brother had just crossed that line I told him not to cross. Trust is Ery Thing and now he has to pay.

"Come on Kaí, I'm out front." (CLICK)

"Dag Dad, you said you would be here in 20 minutes."

"Oh my fault, so you goin out wit Lay mom?"

"Yeah, is it cool wit you?"

"Yeah, do ya thing. Oh, so that's why you brought out ya Maybach?"

"You know how I do; you only get one chance to make a first impression."

"And believe me Dad, you gon' make a hell of a first impression wit this car alone."

I brought out my platinum on platinum Maybach wit tha dub dueces. By tha time I got to my aunt Rose's crib I was hungry as hell. We walked in to be greeted by my little cousin Shy and tha smell of fried fish.

"Kai, Uncle Jerz," she said runnin to us.

Shy was only 5' but she was bad as Shit; my aunt came out of tha kitchen givin me and my dad a hug.

"Well look what tha wind blew in?" We took a seat on tha couch while we were talk'n Bugsy came in.

"Mom who's driving that Maybach out front?"

Then he seen us, "Damn Unc that's how you doin it in DE? Must be nice to be you." I didn't trust Bugsy, especially not after what Reek had told me.

"What up Kai?"

"Sup, what y'all visiting?"

"Nah, I'm movin in wit y'all."

"Oh yeah, you must be sleep' in Reek's room."

"Nah, I was think'n bout taken ya room."

Shy said, "He ain't never here anyway."

"Well then, that's where I'll be."

"Yeah a'ight, you gon' take what comes wit it." I stood up.

"What comes wit it!"

"Y'all two better chill out."

"Nah Ma, he thinks he so tough. Imma show him!"

"You must of forgot what happen last time you tried to show me." As he was about to say something Reek walked in.

"Hey there go my peeps." I could sense that something was going on.

"Well, you better put ya peeps in line for he get hurt up in here."

"Nigga you ain't gon' do nuffin but keep yap'n ya gums."

"Listen here," my unc said stand'n up, "y'all family save that Shit for them cats in tha street. If y'all got a problem wit each other I got some boxing gloves in my trunk."

"Go get 'em Dad so I can teach this dude some respect."

"Nah Unc, I don't do no fight'n," he said lift'n his shirt so his pistol could be seen.

"I heard that," I said now exposing tha 40 cal. that I had on my waist. I knew my dad wasn't going to say nuffin about my gun since he was tha one that gave it to me.

"I don't care what either of you two say but I know this Shit stops here! Right now understood!" We both nodded.

"I was only joking about tha room he took it to tha heart."

"My bag Cuz."

"We would of had to hop on you in here Bugsy," Shy said laugh'n, her and Bugsy always went at it.

"Shy sit down before I beat ya little butt Boy."

"You ain't gon' do nuffin to my baby," my Aunt Rose said.

"I heard that," Reek said, "anyway Unc you doin it big wit that whip outside and you got it sitt'n. Well, let me call Jean and see if she still want to do dinner."

"Hello."

"Hey there, I wanted to know if you still wanted to do dinner and possibly a movie."

"Sure."

"Ok."

"I'm around my sisters."

"What's tha address? I'll punch it in tha Navi and be right there."

"I'll be ready by tha time you get here." She gave me tha address then hung up.

"Unc I know you ain't talk'n bout Lay's mom?" Bugsy asked.

"Yeah."

"You know she use to..."

Before he could finish my dad was like, "Yeah, she already told me."

"And you still gon' date her?"

"Bugsy you is a Fucken Hater," Reek said, "so what she use to get high, she look better than any broad you ever had or will have even when she was gett'n high."

"Damn Nigga, you act like I'm talk'n bout Sash Mom."

"Fall tha Fuck back Nigga!"

I could see Reek was about to snap so I said, "Let me holla at you Reek." We went upstairs to Reek's room so I could put my things away.

"I don't know what's up wit Bugsy but he got one more time to pop fly. That nigga gon' have tha nerve to show that Bullshit Ass .380 when I'm hold'n this," I said pull'n my 40 cal. out.

"I thought Unc was gon' snap."

"Nah, he gave it to me."

"Oh Shit, what you in tha game a little something but he don't know about it."

"So who do you cop from?"

"Him but I go through E so he get it for tha low. Imma tell him once I get my paper all tha way up."

"Sikaí, Sikaí come on for he start trip'n."

"What's up Dad?"

"I'm bout to roll out, here's a few hundred to hold you down for tha weekend."

"Unc you know I got him; you might as well follow us. I'm on my way around there to pick Sash and Lay up so we can grab a bite to eat."

"A'ight lets got then, don't want to keep Jean wait'n."

We pulled up, I honked for Lay and Sash to come out while my unc got out wit a dozen roses. I was bout to knock on tha door when it opened.

"Sup Lay, is ya mom here?"

"Yup, Mom Jerz is here."

"Nice taste," Sash said, "that's must be where Reek gets it from."

"Well we out."

"Bye and try not to keep my mom out too late."

"Excuse me I am grown, at least last time I checked I was." I couldn't keep my eyes off her Apple Bottom jeans and they did her apple bottom no justice.

"You look even better in person."

"Thank you and so do you."

Damn just look'n at him in his Affliction jeans and shirt had my panties moist.

"Let me put these in some water and I'll be ready to go."

As soon we walked outside we couldn't help but notice Jerz's platinum Maybach sitt'n on chrome.

"Yeah Lay, he definitely gett'n paper. Tha new 6 and this? I need to find my mom a man, I wonder if he has any brothers."

"Girl you crazy."

I climbed in tha back where Kaí was.

"Here this is for you," he said handing me a single rose, "I didn't get you a dozen because I think a single rose is more romantic so I hope you don't mind."

"Not at all," she said as she gave me a kiss.

CHAPTER 12

Stick'n Niggaz My New Profession

"What's up wit you? Why you look'n all mad Nigga?"

"Nah, my faggot ass cousin came up for tha weekend and he was talk'n shit."

"Which cousin?"

"My Uncle Jerz son Sikaí."

"Oh Word Kaí up here for tha weekend?"

"Yeah, he runnin round wit Reek somewhere."

"What's up wit ya uncle, he still doin numbers in Delaware?"

"Yeah he got to be, he had a Maybach out front of my moms."

"Damn, niggaz ain't push'n no shit like that unless they a rapper or actor and ya unc ain't neither so he gett'n paper. We might have to go to Wilmington and do our homework on him."

"Nah, I ain't Fuck'n wit him; I remember tha last time niggaz tried to get at him they still ain't been found and it's been 3 years."

"Them dudes wasn't us."

"I feel you but I ain't mess'n wit him."

"That's all it is then but I am gon' get my brother and a few other niggaz. I think I might make stick'n niggaz my new profession. Let them take tha risk, I just collect tha reward and if we happen to get drugs that's a bonus."

"We can still knock that Shit off Bugsy."

"I'm wit that Shit, I got tha perfect hit for us right now. We gon' have to go to Philly but it's well worth it."

"Then say no more, when you try'n ta go?"

"Let me call Shorty and see what's up. Only thing, we got to break her off 20 stacks."

"If she want 20 than it must be some loot involved."

"She said at least 100g's."

"Shit, well call that Bitch now!"

CHAPTER 13

Jerz and Jean's Date

Once we were outside I went around to tha other side and opened tha door for her. As soon as I got into tha car she said, "Let me find out you're a gentlemen or are you just try'n to impress me?"

"A little of both, is it work'n?"

"I'll let you know at tha end of the night."

"Do you have anywhere particular that you want to eat at?"

"Nah." I pushed in restaurants in my Navi to see what was in tha area.

"Do you like Italian food?"

"I've never ate it except spaghetti and lasagna."

"How bout Japanese?"

"Now that's a different story."

"Well, say no more." I pushed tha Japanese restaurant in and let tha Navi do its job.

When we got there it was a half hour wait; we were finally seated. As we looked thru tha menu tha Teriyaki Steak and Shrimp caught my eye wit a stuffed potato and rice on tha side. Jean ordered tha same but instead of plain rice she got Shrimp Fried Rice. We engaged in small talk until our food came. Damn, I had to admit this food was delicious. We had a lot of things in common. I could tell that she was impressed wit my resume; she probably assumed I was just some dumb hustler wit no education. But I know if that was tha case, she thought very differently now. I paid tha tab and we made our way out of tha restaurant into my car.

"So are you up to a movie or is it too late for you?"

She looked at her watch then laughed, "I guess you forgot about that part."

"And what part is that?"

"Tha part about you being a comedian."

"I heard that. Nah, I was just ask'n since you said you don't get out much. Ya body might be use to going to bed at a certain time."

"Oh I see, well since it's 10 o'clock I guess we can catch a movie. What did you have in mind?"

"It doesn't matter, truth be told, I just wanted to spend more time wit you."

"Well, we don't have to see a movie for that; we could go bowling or go back to my house to watch a movie."

"That sounds like a winner."

"Which one?"

"Both, better yet...how about a movie tonight and bowling if you not busy tomorrow night."

"So are you ask'n me on another date?"

"Yes I am."

"Well in that case, I would love to go."

When we arrived at her crib it was only 10:30, we walked in to find Kai and Lay sitt'n on tha couch watch'n TV.

"Y'all home early," Lay said.

"We were comin to watch a movie but I guess..."

Before she could finish Lay said, "Be our guest, we'll go upstairs so y'all can have some privacy."

On their way upstairs Layla said, "Mom Kai's stay'n tha night, so let us know when y'all done so we can camp out on tha couch."

"A'ight, will do," she said givin Lay that look that said you ain't slick.

When they were gone I said, "Kids think they so slick, don't they know we were kids once ourselves."

We both started laugh'n.

We ended up watch'n American Gangster, that was one of my all-time favorite movies. In tha middle of tha movie I fell asleep, I felt Jean get up only to return wit a quilt. I thought that she was going to put it over me and go to her room but to my surprise, she joined me on tha couch rest'n her head on my shoulder. So, I turned my body so that her head would be on my chest. We both fell asleep that way, I was awakened by my phone at 3:30 in tha morning.

"Yo."

"Damn Nigga, I been hitt'n ya phone all night."

"I was busy, what's up?"

"I got my folk up from D.C., they need 10 and I only got 5 left."

"A'ight, I'll be there in 30 to 40 minutes."

I got up to leave but I made sure I woke Jean up before I did so she could get up and go to her room but she just stretched out on tha couch. So, I gave her a kiss on her forehead and let her know I would call her later.

"Damn, I think I'm in love," I said to myself as I watched him walk out tha front door.

I got up to go to my room, I started to wake Lay up but decided not to. I changed into my nightgown and went into my drawer to pull out my toy. For some reason, this orgasm was tha best one. Shit, I had multiple orgasms. Thanks to Jerz that night I slept like a baby.

"Hello."

"Hey Big Bro."

"What's crack'n Lil Sis."

"Same Shit, we need to holla at you."

"No doubt, give me a few hours and I'll be ready." (CLICK)

"Aye Lay, he said to give him a few hours but I need to holla at you though."

"What's up Sis?"

"I was think'n about leave'n tha game alone, I have more than enough money saved up to last me for years. I was think'n bout opening up a beauty salon and barbershop."

"Are you sure?"

"Yeah, I just don't want to be doin this for tha rest of my life. So, I figured I better get out now and retire while I'm ahead."

"So what are you gon' do? Let Reek take care of ya half?"

"I didn't even think about that. Truthfully, I was hoping that you felt tha same day I did."

"Well, I have thought about it only difference I said I would wait until tha end of the school year."

"I talked to Sanchez about it."

"So did I."

"Then you already know how he feels."

"So then, at the end of tha school year."

"Yup."

"Well, I think you should holla at Reek, let him take over. If he says yes, then we introduce him to Sanchez."

"A'ight, I'll holla at him tonight."

"So what's tha deal wit you and Kaí."

"He said that he talked to his mom and dad about movin up here wit Reek so that we could be closer."

"I've noticed he's up here every weekend."

"Yeah that's my baby. Sash, I love him."

"Have you told him that?"

"Nah."

"Why not?"

"I don't know, I'm afraid he might not feeling tha same way I do."

"You just said he might be movin up here to be closer to you; I think he does."

"I don't know."

"I'll tell you what, I'm goin to talk to Reek about what I need to talk to him about and you need to talk to Kaí to see where tha two of y'all stand."

"Ok."

"Nah, I'm serious Lay."

"Me too Sash."

"Well, I'll see you later," I said as I was walk'n out tha front door.

I peeped my head back in, "I see these two are really lovin each other," referring to Jerz and Ms. Jean.

"I know they spend more time than me and Kaí."

"Well, I'll call you."

"Ok."

"Love you Sis."

"I love you too Sis."

CHAPTER 14
Good News

"Yo Cuz."

"What up Kaí."

"I got some good news."

"What's up?"

"My moms and pops said after tha school year I can move up ya way."

"That's what's up, then we can get this Shit really pop'n."

"Yeah, you know I'm comin to tha table wit something. My money will be up by tha end of school."

"Well, what you look'n like now?"

"I'm up to a little more than a half brick."

"That ain't bad for a few months of grind'n."

"Ask me that same question in 6 months when school is out."

"Damn, hold on Cuz...Yo."

"Hey Sexy."

"What up Lay?"

"You busy?"

"Nah, hold on let me tell Reek I'm gon' holla at him later."

(CLICKS TO THE OTHER LINE)

"Reek, that's Lay Imma hit you later."

"A'ight Lil Cuz."

"Hello."

"Damn I ain't Envogue."

"Oh you got jokes."

"So what's up?"

"Nuffin, I got some good news for you."

"Oh yeah and what's that?"

"My moms and pops said that I can move up there after tha school year is over."

"Are you serious?"

"Yup."

"Damn, that's what's up."

"You gon' get tired of me Lay?"

"Nah, I love you too much for that." I tried to throw that in to see what he would say.

"Damn, did Ms. Layla Jackson just say that she loves me?"

"Yes I did, I love you Sikai."

"That's what's up. Damn Lay, I love you too."

"Do you really?"

"One thing I know is never tell a woman that you love them if you really don't. I would never play wit ya feelings and I hope that goes both ways."

"Listen Kai, I was scared to tell you because I didn't think that you would feel tha same. We haven't been talk'n for a real long time. But 7 months is long for me."

"For me to Lay, I've never even had a girlfriend...that's tha truth."

"Oh, so you something like a playa huh?"

"Nah not at all, I just neva found that special girl until I met you."

"Well, I guess it was a good thing we both were on South Street that day huh?"

"Yeah, I guess so."

"So did you really think I was somebody else or was that ya game?"

"Nah, I really thought you were somebody else; I would never use no corny pick up line like that. Damn Lay, give me a little credit."

Since neither of us wanted to hang up, we talked until we both ended up fall'n asleep on tha phone.

"Hello."

"Hey Baby."

"Hey Sexy, you busy?"

"Nah, I was actually gett'n ready to call you."

"Oh were you?"

"Yeah."

"Well, come open tha door, I'm out front."

"OK."

"Damn, took you long enough."

"I was just gett'n out tha shower."

"Damn, I missed that."

"Ain't nuffin you hadn't seen before."

"I know that's right. Where Ms. Shirl?"

"Boy it's 10 o'clock, you know she in bed."

"I should have brought a change of clothes, I could have went to school from here. Fuck it, Imma just rock this again."

"Yeah right, they'll be talk'n bout that."

"I don't care."

"Well, I do... ain't nobody gon' be talk'n bout my baby."

"Matter fact, I got a pair of black cargo pants, a white Tee, and my black ACG Boots in my trunk, not to mention brand new socks and boxers; so I'm set."

"Sounds like you up to no good if you ask me."

"Nah Sash, I only got eyes for you. I thought you would know that by now, but I guess you don't."

"Aye, I know you love me but I do need to talk to you Reek about something real serious. Me and Lay are done wit tha game at tha end of tha school year. If you want to take over, we're will'n to introduce you to our big bro Sanchez. I already told him about you and that me and Lay are done in 6 months."

"Well, y'all must have a nice piece of money to be gett'n out tha game."

"We gon' open a beauty/barber salon."

"Lucky for y'all me and Kaí can cut."

"Yeah alright."

"Nah for real."

"Do y'all?"

"Yeah as a matter fact, I need a shape up now so when we come up this weekend I'm going to let him hit my thing up so you can see his work."

"Well, that ain't gon' do us no good, he only gon' be around for tha summer."

"Nah, after this school year he movin up there for good."

"He just want to be by Lay."

"Yeah, you would say that but that is a part of it. Plus, we gon' turn New Jersey out."

"I know he ain't gon' start you late."

"He already does."

"Damn, let me find out."

"Shit, I just did about a month ago. He said he been at it for 2 months now and he up to a little more than half bird."

"Oh that Shit in y'all blood. Does Jerz know?"

"Nah, he said he was goin to tell him after he was done school this year but I think he already know what's going on. He just wait'n on Kaí to tell him."

"Well, you know Jerz score from Sanchez too."

"Yeah."

"Damn, small world huh?"

"You think."

"Well, you might as well introduce us both then cause it's me and him. Let him know we don't want no handouts. What we come to tha table wit is what we want by June. We'll be grabbing at least 20 or more."

"Well, I'm gon' call Sanchez in tha morning to set up a meeting Saturday."

We talked until we both fell asleep in each other's arms.

CHAPTER 15
A Good Sting

"Are you sure that there's only 3 people in there?"

"Yeah, here's tha vest and badges you'll need. Let me give you a heads up, they might start to shoot. So don't be afraid to shoot back."

"You must don't know who you talk'n to; we live for this Shit Shorty."

Once we were ready we headed to our destination ready for whatever came our way.

"Slim, is she sure there's going to be a hundred grand up in there?"

"She said it is...park right in front."

We got out, walked to tha front door. I listened to see how many voices I could hear; I only heard two people.

I whispered to Slim, "I only heard 2 people so make sure you keep your gun drawn."

"You ready?"

"Yeah." Wit one hard kick tha door flew open.

"Police! Everybody down!"

Tha two guys did as they were told. I could hear tha toilet flush'n so I motioned for Slim to hold them while I went upstairs. I ran to where I heard tha toilet, kicked opened tha door, then yelled, "Police!" As soon as I seen him pull his piece I let one go. (BOOM) was all you heard. He had a big hole where his chest once was. Then I heard 3 shots downstairs. By tha time I got down there tha other two dudes were dead as well.

"What was tha other shot I heard?"

"He tried to pull but wasn't fast enough, that was his finger just react'n off of my blast to his dome."

"Well, get ery thing while I get what's upstairs."

It looked to be about a brick in tha bathroom. I searched tha other 2 rooms as well which were empty. I was walk'n down tha hall when I noticed what looked like an attic so I reached up and pulled tha latch causing it to come down I walked up tha steps wit my shotty drawn. When I got to tha top it was empty except for a trunk that had a lock on it. I used tha end of my shotty to break tha lock. After a couple tries, it finally gave way. When I lifted tha top, I couldn't believe it. I yelled for Slim to bring tha duffle bag. Once I had emptied tha trunk, we made our way to tha truck. We were in and not a minute too soon. I could hear tha sirens in tha distance. I pulled off slowly not to bring any unwanted attention. We checked into a motel, once we had dumped tha stolen truck we had I wanted to tally up what we had. While we were count'n ery thing up Slim's phone began to ring.

"Yo."

"Yeah, we'll be right there." (CLICK)

"All that Bitch gett'n is her 20 grand she asked for."

"Nigga you ain't got to tell me."

When we finished we ended up wit a half mill and 10 bricks. If I didn't know it before I knew it now, I was a Stick-Up Kid. And Slim's girl or whatever she was, would be tha one to help us set niggaz up. So we decided to hit her wit 50g's instead of 20 which she was more than happy about. We let her know that we would be in touch soon.

"And don't go spend'n ya money all crazy either."

"Boy I got this, I ain't no fool."

"By tha time y'all call, I'll have another score set up, something better."

"It can't get no better than this," I thought to myself.

Tha ride back to Jersey was a quiet one, we both were probably wondering tha same thing. What we're gon' spend our money on. I figured I would sell my 5 bricks for 20 a piece so I could get rid of them fast. Shit, especially wit everybody sell'n them for 32 and better. I'm cool wit gett'n a 100g's for them. So that was a good sting, I came out wit 325g's. Hell, that's more doe than I ever seen. I put tha word out and all 10 were gone in 4 days.

Now, where did Slim and Bugsy get work from that they were sell'n bricks for 20 a pop. I know they had to rob somebody not to mention that they were driving around in brand new whips since they were on tha come up. It was time to put my plan into action, I knew where their so-called Stash House was. I had followed them both on more than one occasion just to make sure that they didn't have another spot and they always ended up at tha crib. Tonight would be tha night that I would see how much these dudes was actually work'n wit. I had overheard my brother tell'n my mom about a concert that was goin on in Philly and that he and Slim bucked up on front row tickets. If I'm not mistaken I think he said that tha show started at 9 o'clock but they wanted to get there by 8:30. I called Spit to get him to call Bugsy to see if they had already left. He confirmed that they were already in route to Philly so I let him know to meet me at Old Man Smitty's house in 15 minutes. When he arrived he was ready to go wit his all black on; he pulled out two mask.

I had to laugh, "Where did you get these from?"

"I know some people that know some people."

"That's good enough for me."

We got into tha car that I had gotton from a fiend for a 16th of cocaine for tha night. I drove to tha house they had been goin to we parked around tha corner, put our gloves, and Barack Obama Mask on. I knocked on tha door first to make sure there wasn't nobody home. When no one answered, I used my crowbar to pry tha door open so not to make a lot of noise. We went in and ram sacked tha whole house.

"Spit remember always think like a criminal," I said opening tha freezer and pulling out tha French fry bags, "you see what I'm talk'n bout?"

As I emptied tha bags, I watched tha money fall out. Then I went to tha deep freezer and took out ery thing to find more money underneath all that food. Tha average nigga would never have took all that food out. We put tha money in a bag and left tha same way. We came in quietly not taking our mask off until we got back to tha car. We got back to Old Man Smitty's and counted our take which totaled 300g's. I hit Spit wit 150g's and let him know not to spend it for a minute so he would not draw attention.

"Aye Reek, who's crib was that?"

"It was Bugsy and Slim's."

"Why did we hit ya brothers crib?"

"Remember when he had that Fire a few months back."

"Yeah."

"Well, he broke in here and took my shit because on some Real Shit Spit I don't need tha doe. I just want him to see how it feels. I rather do this than what I was gon' do to them," I said giving him that look to let him know what I meant.

My phone started to ring, "Hello."

"What up Cuz?"

"What you up to?"

"Nuffin, just handled that chick I was tell'n you bout."

"Damn you had to knock her off wit out me."

"Huh?"

"Don't worry about it, I got $75 for you on tha strength that I knocked her off wit out you. I had to though, her parents went out for tha night."

"You still comin up tomorrow?"

"Yeah, either my dad gon' bring me or Lay gon' come scoop me up."

"Did she talk to you yet?"

"Talk to me bout what?"

"If you have to ask then she didn't holla at you yet. I'll let her tell you."

"Awe Nigga, now you gon' have me wonder'n."

"She'll tell you so don't go say'n what Reek talk'n bout? You got to tell me something?"

"Damn, you think that's what I do?"

"All I'm gon' say is..."

"Wow, I never would have thought it would be you of all people."

"Come on Kaí, stop try'n to play me."

"That's how I just felt."

"You right, my bag Little Cuz."

"Damn, you talked her up, I'll see you later."

"A'ight, so you should be straight now."

"Yeah I'm more then straight, I'm gon' spend all mine on some cocaine."

"Well, you might as well let me hold on to it for you."

"I'm gon' holla at my peeps in a week so I'll let you get it at tha number

I get 'em for."

"That's a bet." I counted out 10g's and handed it back to him.

"What's that for?"

"Something to hold you down, go buy yaself a squader for about 2500."

"Nigga I ain't got no license to get no car."

"Damn you ain't got no aunts or uncles that will sign for you?"

"I don't know, my aunt might do it but she always want money."

"So what? You bout to get major paper. A few hundred ain't gon' make or break you."

"Yeah, I guess you right."

"I did see this Crown Vic, I said when I got enough doe I was gon' grab."

"Matter fact, you can buy my shit for 7500 if you want it."

"What ya Park Ave?"

"What other car do I have? I'm bout to spend my half on a whip."

"You gon' do that so soon?"

"Yeah because I already got money; it won't matter if I buy a new whip or not."

"Yeah, I guess you're right. Well, Imma holla at my aunt to see if she will put tha car in her name."

"Check this out Spit, I'll let you keep tha car and insurance in my aunts name on 2 conditions."

"What are they?"

"One, you have to pay tha insurance on time every month."

"Cool, not a problem."

"And two, don't be doing no dumb Shit in it cause that Shit will fall back on my aunt."

"Come on Reek, you ain't got to worry bout no Shit like that wit me."

"A'ight then, you get it after I find me a new whip and you need to go to Motor Vehicle to apply for ya license."

"No doubt, Imma do that in tha morning."

"Well, I'm bout to handle some business so I'll holla at you in tha a.m."

I walked outside to my car to find a note on my windshield that read:

I guess you been busy all day. So when you find tha time stop by.

Love Ya Wifey

All I could do was smile, *"Damn, I haven't talked to my baby all day and I was in need of some lovin."*

After I made a few runs I went by Sash's house. I didn't have to knock on tha door because Ms. Shirl was on her way in. Sash was chill'n in tha front room watch'n reruns of Def Comedy Jam, her face lit up when she seen me walk in wit tha box of pizza.

"You must of been read'n my mind cause Damn I'm hungry."

"Well you out of luck, it's only enough for me and Ms. Shirl."

"Boy you better stop play'n as hungry as I am."

"How many slices do you want?"

"Two please and can you bring me a spring water?" Ms. Shirl took her pizza and went upstairs.

"So what's been up wit you today?"

"Nuffin, just gave Bugsy a taste of his own medicine."

Then I filled her in.

"Reek I don't want you to get hurt."

"Nah Baby I'm cool, it's either I did that or I would have killed them niggaz on some Real Shit."

"Well, you about to really be in charge so just be careful.

"Yo Slim that was a nice concert, tha boy Hov snapped."

"Yeah, but I was really feel'n that nigga Lil Wayne."

"Where you stay'n at tonight?"

"At tha spot."

"Me too."

We pulled up at tha house, as we were walk'n towards tha house I could see tha door ajar. I pulled my gun and so did Slim. When we got to tha door, I pushed it tha rest of tha way open and stepped in guns drawn. Once we made sure no one was in there, I went back to tha kitchen where tha Stash was at.

"Shit! Fuck!" I yelled at tha top of my lungs, "who could have did this! How could anyone know where we live! Somebody is gon' pay for this Shit!! Now we back to square Fuck'n one! I can't believe this Shit! I guess it's true what they say karma is a Bitch!"

CHAPTER 16
D.B.D. tha Code

"Kaí you ready?"

"You can go head, Lay on her way to get me. We got something to do."

"A'ight then, hit my phone later."

"A'ight."

(CLICK) No soon as I hung up my phone started to ring.

"Yo."

"Hey Babe, I'll be pull'n up in 5 minutes."

"I'm on my way out tha door now."

I hopped in tha car, we were going to Philly to finish up Christmas shop'n; I only had to get Lay and my mom something. My dad didn't celebrate holidays because he was Muslim; he had wanted me to convert but I wasn't ready. When I did it, I wanted to do it for tha sake of Allah and nothing else. I didn't know how I was going to get Lay's gift while she was wit me. I had gotton her a diamond necklace and bracelet that said **"MS JACKSON"** in diamonds. Since she already had a chain that said Layla, I only had to give Tony another $1800. He had called me two days prior to let me know it was done. I just had to slip in without her knowing.

"Baby, I got to use tha ladies room."

"A'ight, Imma run next door to holla at Tony real quick." That was perfect timing.

"Kaí what's tha deal?"

"We got to make it quick."

"What's tha rush?"

"She's wit me."

"Oh I see." I gave him tha doe.

"Got my stuff? And put it and tha other bag I had."

"You didn't even look at it."

"I trust you; I know it's official."

"Kaí you ready?"

"Yeah."

"Hold up, let me show you tha piece ya dad is gett'n. He went to tha back and came back wit an icy and I mean icy DB.

He smiled and said, "I still have to put tha other 'D' on it, nice ain't it."

"Yeah, my dad snap wit that? I know he paid a grip."

"Nah, only 35g's."

Lay said, "Only."

"That's chump change to him."

"I know tha bracelet is a sick 50g's."

"Damn is it done?"

He went to tha back and came back wit it. That Shit was sick, it had D.B.D. in 4 spots in all ice. Lay wanted to know what D.B.D. stood for.

"I been wanted to ask you that when I first seen it on ya hand."

"Death B4 Dishonor, my dad's best friend died by that code. A'ight Tony I'll get at you."

"Hopefully you'll give me tha chance to make a piece for you." We turned and walked away.

I didn't know what to get Kaí but Tony just answered tha question for me. It wasn't gon' cost 35g's but I was willing to spend 10 on my baby.

"Hold up Lay, Tony let me use ya bathroom."

"Go head."

While he was in there I let Tony know that I wanted him to make Kai a chain wit D.B.D. and I had 10 stacks for him.

"I need it by his birthday which is tha 23rd of next month."

"You sure? I can have it by Christmas which is 2 weeks away. Matter of fact..."

"Yeah?"

"I'll get him a bracelet made for his birthday." I hurried up and pulled out 5 stacks.

"I'll hit you wit tha rest when I come to pick it up."

"No problem."

"What y'all talk'n bout?"

"Ya dad's chain."

I lied but I knew he would go for it we went into tha Gallery bought a few things, then made our way back to Jersey.

On tha ride I let him know about tha meet'n wit Sanchez tomorrow. He let me know he was down wit it when we pulled up to my house.

Kai said, "I see my dad is here," point'n at tha Benz truck that was parked across tha street.

He and my mom had been seeing each other for about 2 months now. It was a good look; he had my mom happy. I haven't seen her like this since my dad was alive; it made me feel good to see her happy again.

"POLICE! EVERYBODY DOWN! DO IT AND I'LL BLOW YA HEAD OFF!!!"

While I held them at bay, Slim put tha restraints on all 5 of them then proceeded to search tha house. Once we were satisfied, we put our findings in a bag then headed out. It was nowhere near our first take; we only got a 150 grand and 1½ bricks of heroin. We decided to hit Mandy wit tha work since neither of us knew anything about heroin, but we later found out that you could make over a half mil off what Mandy had. She had given it to her brother who in return only hit her wit 200 grand, but she was cool wit that. She had gotten more than us and we did all tha work. She let us know that she would have something else for us in about a week or two.

"Hello."

"Hey Reek."

"What up Lay."

"Are y'all ready?"

"Yeah, we were just about to come thru. I'm waiting on Kaí to get off of tha toilet."

"Eel, like I needed to know that. Well, just meet us at Hometown Buffet in 30 minutes."

"A'ight, got you." As soon as I was putt'n tha phone down Kaí came out of tha bathroom.

"You ready? Lay just called, we got to go."

"Let's go then." When we got downstairs Shy wanted to know if we could take her to tha store.

"Not right now Shy, I have to go somewhere. I'll take you when I come back...OK?"

"Yeah, where y'all going? To get me a Christmas gift?"

I pointed to tha tree then asked, "Don't you think you got enough gifts?"

She smiled and said, "You can never have enough gifts." We walked out tha door laugh'n our asses off.

"Reek I really like this new whip."

"Thanks, I had to step my game up a notch. I can't let my girl out shine me, now can I."

"Has Sash seen it yet?"

"Nah." He had tha new Denali black on black sitt'n on 30s wit tha works.

"I got my permit, let me push this."

"You ain't got no damn permit." I went into my back pocket to get my wallet so I could show him.

"Damn Lil' Cuz so what you get ya L's in 10 days?"

"Yeah, what kind whip you plan on gett'n."

"None, Imma push my pops 600."

"I heard that," he said gett'n out tha drivers side so that I could drive.

I turned tha ignition and headed out. When we pulled up, Sash and Lay were sitt'n in Sash's truck so I pulled up next to them.

When they looked over I read their lips, so I rolled down tha window and said, "Damn what? That's how ya dad doin it?"

"Nah, this Reek Shit."

Sash frowned her face then said, "Show Off."

Causing Reek to smile at her and say, "I still love you." We all got out and went inside.

"4?" tha waitress asked.

"No 5."

"Follow me."

As we were about to be seated this Black man walked up and said, "Is this seat taken?"

I was about to say something when Lay said, "Hey Brother."

I then knew this was Sanchez, he sure didn't look Spanish, but once he really started to talk I knew that he had to be Cuban.

Sash said, "Sanchez this Reek and Sikaí." He extended his hand which we both shook wit out hesitation.

"So you are tha two I've heard lots about."

"All good I hope."

"Don't worry, if it was not you would not be sitt'n here today," he said wit a big smile but I knew exactly what he meant by that, "you see, I have grown to love these 2 ladies as if they were my sisters and even though they choose to leave tha game, I will always love and protect them no matter what."

"Well then, we have one thing in common already," I said wink'n at Lay.

"I also have to agree wit you on that," Reek added.

"Now that were clear on that, let me ask you a question. Sikaí, if you don't already know, I do a great deal of business wit your father so why don't you deal wit him?"

"Well Sanchez, I don't want to be given anything, I want to work for what ever I get so I can say I did it on my own. My father doesn't know that I am in this business and if it's a'ight wit you, I'd like to keep it that way until tha end of tha school year."

Wit a smile on his face he said, "You are just like your dad and that's a good thing but I have to say this, I won't tell him but if he was to ask me I won't lie to him either because Trust is Ery Thing. Wit out it, you have nothing."

"I definitely respect that and you don't ever have to worry about us if something was to ever go down."

"It's always Death B-4 Dishonor," me and Reek both said at tha same time.

Once we finished and our breakfast and our conversation, we all got up to leave.

"Sash, Lay, can I have a word wit you for a minute?" We walked to tha truck so they could talk.

"What's up Big Bro?"

"Listen, I need to put them through one test just to see if I can really trust them. I'm not going to tell you when or what; I just wanted to give you a heads up." We gave Sanchez a hug and he went on his way.

"So if we may ask, where you 2 headed to?"

"Old Man Smitty's, there is money to be made."

"Well, we on our way to Philly we'll call when we get back."

"I thought y'all were done Christmas shop'n."

"Yeah but I want to get my mom a nice bracelet, if that's OK wit you."

"Hey it's ya money, do you."

We pulled off, "Sash, I wonder what Sanchez has in store for them."

"Yeah, our word should have been enough not to mention that he deals wit Kai's dad."

"Well, I trust him."

"Me too." We parked in tha parking lot on 9th and Market and walked over to Tony's.

"Hello Ladies, may I be of some service?"

"Yeah, is Tony in?"

"Tony!" he yelled to tha back.

When he came up he instantly remembered me.

"Oh Sikaí's lady friend, I just finished ya piece."

He went back into tha back to retrieve it. When he came back I couldn't believe my eyes, it was exactly like tha one he had made for his dad. Just nowhere near as many diamonds but it was hot.

"Damn Lay, that is nice."

"Since it's for Sikaí, just give me 4,000."

"Are you serious, only $4,000?"

I looked at Sash and said, "Along wit tha 5,000 I already gave him."

"Oh, I was gett'n ready to say I better get Reek one."

"Thanks Tony, I'll definitely be seeing you again."

As we were walk'n out Sash said, "Damn, Kaí got my sis all messed up for her to spend 9 stacks on him.

"Um excuse me, but I do love him and since I got it why not spend it. You talk'n, how much did you spend on Reek?"

"Nowhere near that; maybe about 5500." Once we were done wit our shop'n, we made our way back to tha car.

"ATL Club, Yeah, We be up in a club. I see her do her thang. You might wanna rap, but she'll make you sing.

See, I was on her and she was on him.

"This my Shit Kaí"

"Yeah Dream, is that nigga..."

WOOP! WOOP!

"Man, these pigs ain't got nuffin better ta do then mess wit us."

I pulled over and cut tha car off, when he got to tha window I rolled it down.

"License, Registration and ya Insurance." While Reek got ery thing out tha glove box, I got my permit out of my wallet.

"I'll be right back."

He and his partner walked back to tha car. After about 5 minutes, they both came back.

"Could you both please step out of the vehicle. Please step out the vehicle!"

"For what? And what was tha reason for stop'n us?"

"Sir Please, step out of the car. I'm not going to ask again."

"Kaí just do what they want so we can be on our way."

When we did they told us to put our hands behind our backs then put tha cuffs on us and sat us in tha back of their car.

"Who's truck is this?"

"It's my mom's truck Officer."

"Is it alright if we search?"

"Sure, go ahead."

"Reek this is some Bullshit."

"I know, we ain't dirty so we cool."

After a few tha Spanish cop came out tha back wit what looked like a brick of coke.

"Nah that Shit ain't mines."

"You sure you didn't forget it was in there?"

"Hell Nah, I ain't careless."

"They try'n to set us up."

"Well, don't say Shit. My dad will get us tha best lawyers."

When they came back to tha car tha White cop said, "Would one of you like to explain this?"

Before Reek could say anything I said, "I want to call my lawyer."

"That's up to you, follow me to the station." On tha way, he tried to get us to talk or should I say tell.

All I said was, "So what do you think about Obama becoming tha first Black president?" That made Reek smile.

"Damn Cuz, you a'ight? You over there sweat'n bullets."

"Yeah, I'm straight."

We got to this build'n where all these unmarked cars were; he got us out and took us in. Once inside I knew this must be Vice Headquarters. When we got to tha front desk he put our IDs on tha desk and logged us in, then put us in two separate interview rooms. I was tha least bit worried, I just hope that my cuz wasn't one of those weak niggaz because now is tha time we would find out.

After about an hour, tha White cop and one of tha Vice came in.

"So do you want to talk?" I had no idea that Sanchez was behind tha glass watch'n tha whole thing.

"Yeah, I want to talk."

"Well start talk'n."

Just as I was about to go in Kaí said, "Yeah, I want to talk to my lawyer. So before you waste your time and mines wit tha good cop bad cop Bullshit, you might as well let me call my lawyer and I have nothing further to say."

And I put my head down on tha table. They must of knew I was serious because they walked out.

"Damn Sanchez, he ain't gon' talk."

"Now I've been doin this Shit for years and I know when they will fold and that one in there..."

"Unh, Unh...Ok, let's try his cousin out."

They picked up tha brick and headed to tha other interview room. I took my spot behind tha glass, they walked in wit tha brick of coke and dropped it on tha table.

"Now your cousin says this belongs to you."

I didn't say shit, I just sat there. I knew that Kaí had tha same blood as me and he would not sell me out. At least I hope he would not. Anyway, he knew that Trust is Ery Thing and no matter what its always "Death B-4 Dishonor."

"So why does your cousin say this belongs to you and that you just met wit a guy named Sanchez for breakfast along wit 2 females?"

"Oh Shit! He had to talk; how would they know that? Once I make bail I'm gonna have to kill my lil cuz."

"Listen, I don't give two Fly'n Fucks what he told you. I need to call my lawyer and that's all Imma say." They left tha room, I couldn't believe my cuz would fold like that.

"Hey Sanchez, if that didn't do it nothing will. I know he knows we wouldn't have known that."

"A'ight, try it on Sikaí."

"Here we go again. Listen, you Little Fuck, we got you now! Ya so called family gave it all up. He says that this," and pointed to tha cocaine, "belongs to you and that you met a guy named Sanchez along with two females for breakfast this morning."

"Oh Shit! No Reek! How could you tell them that?" I thought to myself, *"I have no choice, I have to kill Reek. Trust is Ery Thing and he has done tha unthinkable."*

"All I have to say is 5 words, let me call my lawyer."

They told me to stand up then led me down tha hall while I was stand'n there they brought Reek. Neither of us said a word, we just stared at one another wit murder in our eyes. When they opened tha door, Sanchez stood before us. We didn't know what was going on.

"Carl uncuff them, I now know that I can trust both of you without a doubt."

"So this was all a test?"

"Yes and you both passed."

"Reek you lucky cause I was gon' kill you."

"Shit! I was gon' kill you cause when they said Sanchez and breakfast I knew you had to talk for them to know that."

"That's tha same thing I thought."

"Well, I knew that if they said that to both of you then you would both think tha other one was talk'n but still you both just said call my lawyer. I'll be in touch wit you and these guys; they work for me. So don't worry." We grabbed tha keys and headed outside.

"Reek take me to tha nearest tattoo parlor. I need to get my other hand done A.S.A.P."

"What you gon' get?"

"T.I.E., Trust is Ery Thing."

"Yeah, me too."

An hour later we had our tattoos, both our phones started ring'n, of course it was Lay and Sash. We filled them in on what had transpired.

"Damn, I can't believe Sanchez did that."

"He didn't do that to us, that's cause José let him know."

"Yeah you right, since his brother was deal'n wit us he knew we were official."

"They didn't even sound upset about it."

"Well, that's probably because they understand what he was doing."

My phone started to ring, I looked at tha caller ID then smiled.

"Hello."

"Damn, you hung up all fast, I wasn't done talk'n."

"Oh, I'm sorry."

"What size does ya mom wear? I wanted to get her something for Christmas."

"She wears tha same size I do and don't be spend'n a whole lot of money on her either."

"Do I tell you how to spend ya money?"

"No."

"Ok then."

"You so damn smart."

"So when do you want to get started on our prom outfits?"

"Well, Lay said that her and Kai were going to New York next weekend to some designer to get their measurements."

"Oh," I said look'n at Kai, "they gett'n their prom Shit made." All he could do was smile.

"Well, I guess we'll be going wit them."

"I was hoping you said that."

"Well, call me when you get back."

"A'ight, so do you know what colors y'all wearing?"

"Yeah, we decided on ivory and pink."

"I think I want to wear white and red."

CHAPTER 17

Stopped By to Unclog My Pipes

"Hey Slim."

"What up Mandy?"

"Nuffin."

"What's on ya agenda for tha night?"

"I can't call it. Why, what's up?"

"I was hoping you would stop by to unclog my pipes for me."

"Yeah, I could definitely do that."

"Ok Daddy, swing by."

"Is an hour good?"

"Yeah, I'll be wait'n for you."

Damn, did I miss that Bomb Ass Sex of his. For tha past few weeks, I had not had sex do to tha jobs I was turn'n him and Bugsy on to. So, to say I was do would definitely be an understatement but that all would change tonight. I had even stopped stripp'n because tha money from tha new job was more than enough to live off of. I even moved out tha projects and brought me a nice 2-bedroom house in tha suburbs. I was beginning to think Slim wasn't going to show, it has been nearly 2 hours and he still hadn't gotten here yet; then I heard keys in tha door. I knew it was Slim because nobody knew where I lived, let alone had keys to my house. When he walked in, I was stand'n in tha middle of tha living room in a pair of black thongs and match'n bra.

"Damn Daddy, I thought I was gonna have to go upstairs and pull out one of my toys."

As soon as I seen Mandy stand'n there in her thongs, I got an instant erection. I couldn't front, Mandy was a Bad Bitch! She was a stallion 5'6, brown skin, hazel eyes, shoulder length hair, and an ass like tha broad who played Lisa Raye's cousin on Playa's Club. Her body was flawless to say tha least, no stretch marks, no cellulite. If she wasn't a stripper I would definitely wife her, but I can't have no wife of mine grind'n on no otha nigga. I don't care how much they pay'n and I know that she's no whore because it took me 3 months to hit. But when I did, it was well worth it, she had ery thing in her favor. Now, here I was staring at this goddess of a woman ready to give her tha best sex of her life especially since I was on "E" (Ecstasy). She walked up to me and tongued me down; all I could do was grab a hand full of ass. I slid her thong down then dropped to my knees. She knew what was next because she opened her legs to let my face in. After about five minutes, I felt her body jerk I knew that she had reached her climax; her 1ST of many more to come. I guided her to tha couch where I turned her around and went to work. Lick'n her from tha back of her neck down to tha crack of her ass causing her to jump. After lett'n her climax again, it was time to head upstairs. Where tonight instead of having sex, I made love to Mandy for tha first time since we have met and I met her almost 2 years ago. She loved every minute of it and for tha first time Mandy said she loved me but I couldn't say it back. Not that I didn't, I just couldn't make a stripper my girl.

Tha next morning, I was woken by tha smell of bacon. I went to tha bathroom to wash up and take care of my hygiene. By tha time I got downstairs breakfast was ready.

"Good morning Daddy."

"Same to you," I replied. We sat down to eat.

"Daddy I meant what I said last nite."

"Baby, you said a lot last night."

"You know what, don't even go there. I'm talk'n bout when I said I love you; I think it's time we stop play'n and become serious."

"Listen Mandy I can't front; I do love you but you know I can't make you my wifey."

"Why, because I use to be a stripper?"

"Damn, did you say..."

"Yeah, I said use to. I haven't stripped in about 3 months; I gave that up. If you wasn't so busy runnin tha streets then you would have known that and I'm not try'n to be smart, I'm just being honest."

"Listen Mandy, any man in their right mind would love to have you as a wife, I just don't know if I'm tha one that will make you happy."

"Slim, you must really not know me, if nothing else you should know that I'm gon' ride wit you til tha wheels fall off and even when they do Imma still ride."

"Say no more, Mandy that's all I needed to hear so unless you change ya mind I do want to be wit you. And if we are gon' to be wit each other then we gon' definitely have to change our living arrangements because I'm gon' need to see ya Sexy Ass first thing in tha morning and tha last thing at night."

"How we gon' work that out? Cause neither of us wants to leave our hometown plus I just bought this house."

"I don't know, we gon' work it out, believe me."

CHAPTER 18

Tha Day Before Christmas

It was tha day before Christmas and they were having a party in Salem, anybody who was somebody was supposed to be in attendance. Me, Reek, Lay, and Kai decided to ride together and why not, we were going to end up leaving together anyway. When we pulled up to tha Elks it was J. Peed and cars were still pull'n up. We found a spot to park and climbed out.

"Damn Boy, I need a ladder to get in and out of ya truck." We all started laugh'n.

We walked around to where everybody who wasn't already in was stand'n in line.

"Sash, Lay!" We looked to see who was call'n us.

"Up here Ahmad!"

"Yeah, come on."

"Let's go y'all."

When we got to tha front Ahmad was stand'n at tha door; we didn't even have to pay.

"What you doin out?"

"This is my cousins party so I figured I'd come out to support him, you feel me."

"Yeah."

"My fault, what up Reek?"

"I can't call it."

"This my cousin Kai."

"What's good?"

"All tha broads in here," Ahmad said.

"Yeah a'ight," Lay shot back. Ahmad looked at me.

"Yeah that's her." (BOOP-BOOP)

"Oh my bag, Lay no disrespect tended."

"None taken, I jus want it to be known he's taken."

"I heard that," Sash said while we were taking a few pictures.

My cousin Drew walked up, "Damn Lil Cuz, I see you all fly wit ya Christian Dior dress on."

"You know how I do."

"Let me take a few flicks wit you and Sash." Kai and Reek moved to tha side.

"Hey Lay, my mans is on ya heels; he keep try'n to get me to holla at you for him but I told him that I don't do tha match maker Shit."

"I'm good anyway, like Mc. Lyte said I got a man and what ya man got to do wit me," I turned around to see Drew.

"Boy all in my space. Excuse you," I said push'n him back.

I looked at Kai but he had his back to us and I'm glad he did. I didn't want no drama like Mary J., but dude was persistent.

"Look, see that guy right there!"

"What about him?"

"Well, that's my man."

"You must not have heard me Ma!"

"What ya man got to do wit me?"

I looked at Drew, "I think ya boy had one too many," I said as I walked away and stood by Kai.

I could hear Sash say, "Drew, tell ya peeps to fall back for some Bullshit get started over nuffin."

"Aye Gabe fall back."

"Nah Drew, tell ya peeps stop front'n and tell this broad mine her business."

Now Reek was walk'n over, "What's up Drew?"

"I can't call it Reek, ya mans a'ight?"

"Yeah, he straight."

"And if I wasn't ain't nobody gon' do Shit to me."

I looked at Drew who gave me that look that said chill so I grabbed Sash's hand and led her to dance floor where we started bump'n to Cassidy's "My Drink N' 2 Step." When "Bust It Baby" came on, Lay and Kaí hit tha floor while they were dancing Drew's boy came up to Lay and turned her around.

"Excuse you," I heard Lay say then turned back around.

"You know dude."

"Nah, that's my cousins peoples. I told him once that I had a man."

He grabbed my ass but before I could say anything Kaí was on him. These other 2 dudes that must of been wit them too jumped in. That's when Reek jumped in and so did Sash. My cousin Drew was try'n to break it up; I picked a bottle up and busted one of tha dudes in tha head causin him to fall. Then me and Sash was on him while Kaí and Reek handled tha other two. When they finally did break it up, tha one I hit wit tha bottle was a bloody mess. Thanks to us, they shut tha party down at 2 o'clock. When we got outside, my cousin Drew told us to get in our car and leave. No soon as we climbed in Reek's truck shots were fired into tha air. Kia and Reek both grabbed their pistols from in tha glove box.

"That nigga shoot'n in tha air!"

Since Reek had that dark tint they didn't even see us ride right pass; within seconds tha cops were everywhere. We went to tha Waffle House to get something to eat before we went in.

CHAPTER 19
It's Christmas Day

Tha next morning my body was so sore, it had been a while since I had got into a fight; I had muscles that were sore that I didn't even know existed. I got out of bed and made my way to tha bathroom to take a nice hot shower. I didn't see Lay so I figured she was downstairs opening her gifts that me and Ms. Jean had gotten her. But when I got to tha bathroom tha shower was already on, I turned to walk away until I heard Lay in there singing Rhiana's "Take A Bow," I knocked on tha door.

"Who is it?"

"It's me." When I heard tha door being unlocked I walked in.

"Good morning and Merry Christmas Baby."

"Well I see somebody's in a good mood this morning."

I washed my face and brushed my teeth. I had been wit Layla almost 8 months and we hadn't had sex yet. Not that we didn't want to, it was that we both respected tha other. I wanted her to make tha first move and vice versa.

As I was about to leave tha bathroom Lay said, "Oh, you not gon' get in wit me?" That caught me off guard totally.

"Do you want me to?"

"I wouldn't have asked if I didn't."

"Well in that case." I started to take off my t-shirt and boxers.

Damn, I have never seen him totally nude before. I figured we have been together almost 8 months; it was time to stop play'n. As soon as he stepped into tha shower, I pulled him to me feel'n his nakedness against my skin which made me horny. I made my way to his penis wit my hands and started to caress it which made it stiffen up wit my touch. We just rubbed each other's bodies then we washed one another up and got out. We would have to finish this in tha bedroom. On our way back to tha bedroom my mom called up to say that she needed to go to tha grocery store to pick up a few things so she could start Christmas dinner and to keep an eye on tha roast that was in tha oven.

"Turn it on low Mom! I was going back to sleep."

"You not gon' come open ya gift up?"

"Yeah."

"When?"

"When I get up."

"Well, I'll just turn it on low; I shouldn't be more than an hour."

"Ok."

I walked into my room, Kai was about to put his clothes on.

"What are you doin?" I asked takin off my towel exposin my body.

"Gett'n dress," was his reply. I walked over to him and pushed him back on tha bed.

"You can do that when we finish, right now we need to take care of some business."

When it was all said and done I was really in love. He threw it on me something serious; it was well worth tha wait. I had sex before but nuffin like that. Don't get me wrong, I knew I had threw it on him just as good. I was gon' make sure he didn't go nowhere any time soon. We both washed up and headed downstairs, my mom had tha house smell'n like a soul food restaurant. You could smell tha mixture of collard greens, macaroni & cheese along wit all tha other food. When I got to tha bottom of tha steps, I was surprised to see Kai's dad wit an apron on in tha kitchen. I looked at Kai.

"Yeah, my dad is something like a chef."

"Hey Jerz, my mom still at tha store?"

"Yeah, she on her way, I told her I would get it started for her."

"Well, you got it smell'n good in this piece."

"Yeah that's what I do; Kai go too."

"Oh do he?"

"Let me find out."

"Kai did you call ya mom?"

"Nah, I talk to her yesterday when I put gifts under tha tree. My mom was gon' get you a gift but I told her you don't do tha Christmas thing."

"I know I felt bad not being able to get her nothing but Imma take her to Bermuda after tha New Year."

"Damn, let me find out you really like my mom. I know Dad you over here more than me." We all busted out laugh'n.

"What did I miss that has everybody laugh'n so hard?"

"Nuffin Mom, just an inside joke."

"Let's go get tha rest of tha bags Kai." As soon as they left I let my mom know that Jerz was really feel'n her.

"Well, I would hope so, we've been dating for tha past 2 months. Not to mention, I'm feel'n him."

"Well, that's all it is."

"Who is it?"

"It's Reek, open tha door." When I did, he had both arms full wit presents.

He walked in, "Ho! Ho! Ho! Merry Christmas!" Reek said as he put tha presents down under tha tree, "hold on Babe I got a few more things to get." He came back wit a big box and two on top.

"Damn."

"This is for ya mom."

"Well then, let me open it."

Mom touched tha box then said, "It's not tha Crocodile I wanted."

"Mom stop being funny and just open it."

As soon as she tore tha wrap'n paper off she ran over to Reek and gave him a big hug. Reek had gotten her tha computer she wanted and tha copier, printer, scanner, fax machine, and surround sound. My mom wasted no time unhook'n tha old one and replacing it wit tha new one.

"Ms. Shirl, you ain't cook?"

"No, we going to Lay's house for dinner."

Sash opened her gifts and couldn't stop smiling. I had gotten her tha Gucci and Prada bag she wanted along wit tha match'n jackets and also this nice ass icy Prada watch.

He looked at me and my mom and said, "Merry Christmas, this is for you."

He opened his stuff and couldn't stop smiling. My mom had gotten him this nice ass leather coat while I got him a few Gucci and Ralph Lauren sweat suits along wit a nice pair of diamond earrings.

"Well I'll be back; I have to give my mom her present."

I parked in front of Old Man Smitty's and got into my mother's present which she badly needed because every other day her Ford Escort was break'n down. I pulled up to my house and went inside, my little sister had so many toys that she didn't know what to play wit first.

When she seen me she jumped up, "Thank you Reek! I love my Dora bike and Power wheels. Did you give Mommy her gift?"

"Oh yeah," she ran and got tha gift from under tha tree, "here Mommy! Merry Christmas!" When my mom opened up her gift her smile said it all.

"I love it! Put it on for me Tyreek." After I put it on I couldn't deny how good it looked. Tony did his thing, a diamond necklace wit a #1MOM charm all ice.

"Thank you Shy," she said but wink'n at me.

"Now for my present Mom."

"Another present?"

"Close your eyes," I whispered to Shy and told her to open tha front door. When she did she let out a loud scream. My mom jumped but I still had my hands on her eyes. When I got to tha door I took my hands off her eyes and said, "Merry Christmas Mom!"

"Oh My God is this mines!"

"Yes, it's all yours."

I had got her an Acura RL and put a big bow on It. My mom was old fashion, it didn't take much to please her that's why I love her so much.

"Where are tha keys?" I handed her tha keys

"Baby, keep an eye on my food, I'm takin my new car for a spin."

"I want to go Mommy."

"Get in tha back and put on your seat belt."

My mom pulled off; I went back in to check on her food. When my mom finally came back she let me know that she loved her new car.

"Reek, why you didn't put no rims on mommy car?"

"Girl you know I don't need all of that."

"We gon' ride in style Mommy."

"Mom, you want a little dub on ya whip?"

"Tyreek I'm not into that, as long as my car runs that's all I need."

"Well, Imma take it to Rocco's in tha morning to get you an alarm."

"Now I'll take that."

"Well, I be back a little later."

"Where is Kaí? I want to thank him for my bracelet and sweat suit."

"He probably over Lay's house."

"Call his cell phone."

"Ok."

"Thank you for tha car Baby."

"I owe you my life Mom." As I was about to leave Bugsy walked in tha front door. Mom said Merry Christmas, his response was Ba Hum Ba.

"If it ain't tha Grinch," Shy said and went back to play'n wit her dolls.

"Well love y'all, see y'all later," I said walk'n out.

When Lay finally got around to opening her gifts she was more than happy. I went back upstairs to get my gift, when I came down I handed her tha gift and she couldn't open it open it fast enough.

When she finally did, all she could say was, "You really love me." I started laugh'n.

She went to retrieve my gift, I immediately opened it; I too was a loss for words.

"I love you!"

"I see it goes both ways," my dad said, "damn, I just got tha same piece made."

"Nah Dad, ya piece had a lot more diamonds."

"It sure did, how you know?"

"Because Tony showed us when I went to get Lay's stuff made. Kaí I seen how much you liked it so I got you one just a smaller version."

"I know it's not like ya dad's super super icy but it's icy fo' sho."

"Lay come here Girl," I said giving her a kiss.

We all sat around laugh'n. For tha next few hours that night, we all ate dinner.

Ms. Shirl said, "Jean you really put ya foot in it this year."

"Yeah, it's jump'n," Reek said.

"Well, I can't take credit for it, Jerz did it all."

"Well, Well, Well let's see...good look'n, extremely nice, and you can cook Jean you better marry this man," we all laughed at that, "so Jerz, do you have any brothers?"

"Nah, I don't only sisters."

Lay looked at me and said, "They say tha apple doesn't fall far from tha tree."

"Girl you a mess."

We all enjoyed our dinner then decided to go to tha Lagoon for tha Christmas party they were throw'n.

CHAPTER 20

Officially Retired from tha Game

"Hello."

"Hey Sanchez."

"Hey Sis, I was start'n to get worried about y'all. I haven't heard from you in about 2 weeks."

"We been busy wit tha shop try'n to get things right for our grand opening in another month."

"So how is it comin along?"

"Great, just great."

"I thought you were gon' wait til June to open?"

"We were but then we decided to open it next month since tha contractors were finished their job. That brings me to tha reason for this phone call, we also decided not to wait until June to stop grind'n."

"I kind of figured that because you haven't called and I have been doing a lot of business wit Reek and Kaí. I'm glad that you have decided to stop and not get caught up in it like a lot of us have, myself included."

"Well, have a good day and I will be in touch wit you and Lay on a regular basis."

"And you do tha same, you know we will love you."

"And I you. I need to call and set up a meet'n wit Reek and Kaí to let them know that Layla and Sasha have officially retired from tha game."

Reek didn't answer, so I tried Sikaí's number. He answered after tha 3rd ring.

"Hello."

"Kaí, how are you My Friend?"

"Who this?"

"You don't know who this is?"

"Nah, who this?"

"It's Sanchez."

"Oh, what you switch numbers?"

"Nah, you don't have this one, set in ya phone."

"Unh, Unh."

"Well, make sure you program it in. I called to say that I need to see you and Reek later today if that is possible."

"No doubt, what time we talk'n bout?"

"It's 2:30 now, how about 6 o'clock at tha Steakhouse?"

"Be there." As soon as he hung up I alerted Reek.

"Yo what up Lil Cuz?"

"Sanchez says to meet him at tha Steakhouse at 6."

"A'ight, where you at?"

"I'm around Old Man Smitty's."

"That's where you gon' be?"

"Yeah, I ain't goin nowhere."

"Cool, I'll be by at 5:30."

Even though we were really start'n to do big numbers, we still pumped dimes. I wonder what my dad is goin to say once I tell him that I'm in tha game because by tha way things are going I'll be crazy up by June. In a way, I do want to tell him now but Reek said I should just hold off. I ended up dozing off, I didn't realize I was sleep that long until Black and Fire started bark'n at tha door. It was like they knew Reek's scent.

He peeked in, "Damn Nigga get up, I know you heard me beep'n tha horn."

"Nah, actually I was in here knocked out on tha couch sleep."

"Well, get ya ass up. It's 5:45 and I'm not try'n to be late."

"Here I come."

On tha way there Reek asked me what I wanted to do for my birthday in 2 weeks.

"I don't know, I was think'n about rent'n a hall and having a party."

"I was gon' ask you if you wanted to have a party. Don't worry Lil Cuz, I got you. We gon' do it big."

"Aye Reek."

"I got 2 extra tickets to tha Nets and Sixers game if you and Sash want to go wit me and Lay."

"I didn't know Lay like basketball."

"Yeah, she likes all sports, Sixers is her squad. Imma die hard New York fan even though we been out of contention for damn near a decade now. Shit, we ain't did nothing since tha lock out season when we went to tha finals and lost against tha Spurs. But wit all that said, at tha end of tha day I'm still a die-hard NY Knicks fan."

"I heard that, I'm a Lakers fan myself but I'll ask Sash and see what she says. She's not into tha sports thing."

"I heard that."

"Matter fact, nah Cuz Imma pass...why don't you take Ms. Jean and ya dad."

"Yeah, we can make it a family affair."

He started laugh'n, "Kaí you crazy." When we pulled up Sanchez was just getting out of his car; we parked and did tha same.

"Good evening."

"3?"

"Yeah."

"Follow me please." Tha waitress led us to a secluded booth in tha back.

"I'll be back to take ya orders but can I get you something to drink?"

"Yeah, 3 spring waters."

"Ok, I'll be right back."

"Sanchez, I thought you lived in Spanish Harlem?"

"I use to but I had to move, I couldn't live that close to business so I brought a nice home in Newark, New Jersey. Well as you probably know, Sash and Lay have stepped away from tha game earlier than planned so are you ready to fully run tha show?"

"Listen Sanchez, not to sound big headed but we make money, money doesn't make us; it's in our blood."

"Yes, I know so tha price is 10g's a brick. I know that you only want a few until you get ya money up but I am will'n to front you whatever you want to help you get into position."

"Well, we can start off wit a light 20 and tha next time we will more than double."

He put us down wit how ery thing is gon' to work. We also let him know that we needed tha 20 A.S.A.P., truth be told, they were already sold.

He said, "By tha time we finished they would already be in play, just make sure to call a day in advance. So, if you wanted more tomorrow, you would call today to place ya order." We finish talking and eating then went our separate ways.

By 11 o'clock, I was on tha phone wit Sanchez.

"Hello."

"Kai is ery thing a'ight."

"Yeah, ery thing is straight, you said to call a day in advance."

"You done already?"

"Just about, I wanted to know if tha shop on 54th Street would be open tomorrow?"

"You said 54th?"

"Yeah."

"Well, they will be open at 8 or 9 o'clock tomorrow morning."

"Ok, I'll see you then."

When I hung up my peeps from down Sussex hit me wanting to know what tha numbers were look'n like. Since we were still in recession, I normally charge them 12,600 for 9 on a regular day so I just let them know that tha numbers were still tha same for them. He wanted to know if he could get tha 2 for 100g's flat. I let him know he could slide this time, Shit I was get'n 10 for that price. He said he would be up at 10 in tha morning which was fine wit me as long as his money was right. I called Lay to see if she wanted to ask her mom and my dad if they wanted to go since Reek and Sash had other plans. I could hear her ask'n her mom if she wanted to go to tha game.

"Kai what's up, she said that we have to ask Jerz because they were going out for dinner."

"Well tha game don't start til 8 o'clock, we can all go eat then slide to tha game unless they wanted to be alone."

"Hold up, ya dad just walked in, let me see what...he says that we can do dinner and tha game."

"A'ight, I'm on my way."

"NOBODY MOVE! POLICE!"

BONG! BONG! BONG! BONG! BONG! BONG! BONG! BONG! BONG! BONG! BONG! BONG! BONG! BONG! BONG! BONG! BONG! BONG! It was like a shoot-out, but when it was all said and done there were 3 dead dudes and Slim had gotten grazed in tha arm. But to hear him tell it, 300g's and 3 bricks was well worth it. On tha break down we got 125g's and a brick apiece; Mandy got tha remainder.

"So Slim, you finally decided to get wit Mandy huh?"

"Yeah, well I guess T-Pain said it best I'm in love wit a stripper."

"Cut tha Bullshit Bugsy," she ain't been strip'n for about 4 months now."

"Oh yeah?"

"Yeah, she got a job at tha bank."

"Did you say tha bank?"

"Yeah," I saw that look in his eyes.

"Don't even think about it. That Shit has more security than a little bit."

"Oh, so you must have already been doing ya homework."

"You better know it, they got that shit tighter than a virgin."

"What bank is it?"

"First National."

"No wonder, it's tha biggest bank in Philly. We would be fools to try them. Real rap.

"Slim my brother eat'n crazy, I think he due to get hit again."

"Bugsy you just don't give a a Fuck! You don't have no conscience."

"Nigga neither do you, if either of us had one we wouldn't be stick'n niggaz for they hard earned money." I had to laugh at that one.

"So you really want to rob Reek again?"

"Yeah, but I was think'n about kidnapping my little cuz and hold'n him for ransom."

"Then that's going to involve ya uncle."

"Shit, I didn't consider that."

"I know you didn't."

"That's even better, we can get a lot of paper off this. Let me map this all tha way out for a few months."

"Since we will be play'n wit fire I just hope we won't get burnt in tha process."

"Nigga stop wit all that worrying. Let me plan this out carefully so we don't Fuck this up! It's going to be our biggest sting yet."

CHAPTER 21
Two Days Before Kaí's Birthday

It was two days before Kaí's birthday and Tony called to say that his bracelet was done. Since his dad wanted me to help him pick out a car he said he would take me to get it. When we got up there, as usual there wasn't anywhere to park.

After 20 minutes we finally found somewhere to park. We walked inside to find Tony runnin game on some dude. As soon as he seen us he stopped his conversation wit tha dude he was talk'n to and came over to us.

"What it be like," he said wit his hand out for Jerz to shake.

"You know, same Shit just a different day."

"You here to pick up tha tennis bracelet?"

"Damn, I had totally forgot about that but since I'm here you might as well bring it out too," then he looked at me and said, "hello Layla, please forgive my rudeness."

"It's OK Tony, I understand when a lot of money is in front of you," I said point'n to Jerz, "you forget about tha little," referring to myself.

"Nah Tony, say it ain't so."

"All money is good money to me; you should know that."

"I guess I should."

"Hold on, I'll be right back." When he came back he had both bracelets, I was impressed wit both.

"Do you think ya mom will like it?"

"Who wouldn't like that wit all those diamonds and I'm sure Kaí is going to love his as well."

We paid Tony and were our way to Delaware to tha car lot. We ended up pick'n out a cranberry on cream wit cranberry pipen 09 S600. It just hit tha showroom floor, it had 10 miles on it.

All I could say was, "Wow!" Tha guy Matt that sold it to us knew Jerz from doing business wit him.

"What are you gon' do wit ya other one?"

"Nah Matt, this for my son, his birthday is in 2 days."

"Oh I see, are you pay'n it off today?" I looked at him.

"My fault, dumb question."

I couldn't believe it, if I didn't know now I did. Jerz was caked up, I didn't know that he had four cleaning services that were doin extremely well. He was a very smart man; I gained a lot of respect for him today. Not that I already didn't, but I had a lot more.

"Lay, do you think I should put tha works on it or let him do it?"

"Nah, you should put it on it for him. My peeps Rocco will do tha damn thing."

"Is he expensive? Cause I got some peeps too."

"Nah not for me, I got you." After tha paperwork was done Matt drove off tha showroom floor.

"Lay you can push Kai's 6, I'll follow you." By tha time we made it to Rocco's I was starving and I let Jerz know it.

"Damn, you ain't gotta say it like that, I'll treat you to McDonalds." I gave him that look that said yeah right.

But instead I said, "So I look like a Micky D's chick huh?"

"Naw, I was just joking wit you but we can go somewhere to eat you like Olive Garden."

"No."

"Well, how about TGI Fridays?"

"Now you talk'n, Rocco said he would call us when he was done." While we were eat'n both our phones started ring'n; we looked at one another and started smiling.

"Hello," we both said.

"Hey Baby, nuffin, having lunch wit Jerz."

"Hey Sexy, nuffin having lunch wit Lay. We went to Philly so she could pick up Kai's gift then we went and picked him out a car. Yeah, I'll be there when we finish eat'n."

"What you say Kai?"

"Oh nah, he was giving me a few ideals on tha beauty salon/barbershop. I'll see you in a few."

"Speak'n of that, when are you and Sash opening up?"

"Our grand opening is next week. Do you want to see tha Layout?"

"Yes."

We finished up then headed to tha shop. When we got there, Sash and Kweet one of tha stylist were walk'n in so we followed suit.

"Wow, I really like this."

They had 4 flat screens hang'n from tha corners so that everybody could see them. Tha place was big, on one side it was tha barbers and tha other was tha stylist. There were 8 stylist and 6 barbers, 8 if you included Reek and Kai.

"So are you and Sash going to be doin hair also?"

"Yeah, we didn't get our license for nuffin."

"I heard that Girl," Sash said high five'n Lay.

"Stylz & Cutz is goin to knock off all tha competition, we got tha top stylist and barbers from here to Philly."

"Well, tha layout is nice, especially tha game room in tha back."

"Yeah, cause not everybody can find a babysitter so bring them wit you and we got somebody to monitor them."

I liked tha way they had their names on their mirrors. I could tell that they were going to do numbers once everybody got wind. Rocco had called to say he was done. When we got back to his shop I was jealous, Kaí's whip was off tha chain to say tha least; his 22s really brought out his car. I asked Rocco if I could leave it here for a few days which he said yeah. I even offered to pay but he refused to take my money. After all tha money I had spent on tha rims, system, alarm, and automatic start who could blame him.

I had given out flyers all over Jersey and Delaware for tha party I was throwing Kaí at tha Chase Center down tha Riverfront in Wilmington. I even sent out a bulletin to ery body on Facebook as well as Instagram. Here it is 2 days before tha party and I still don't have my outfit done yet, but I know if Sam said he would have that done in time then he would. I let Kaí talk me into gett'n a Prada shirt and blazer made because he had his dads peoples make him tha same Shit back but wouldn't let me see it. Which was definitely understandable cause I would be tha same way.

"Hello."

"What's up Lil Cuz?"

"I can't call it Reek."

"Just got out of school, can't wait to walk and get that diploma."

"Tired of school?"

"Yeah and no, for tha past week in a half All everybody has been talk'n bout is my party at tha Chase Center.”

“Yeah, it’s in 2 days. Well, is ya gear ready?”

“Nah, Sam said later today. Since my party is down here I won’t be up this weekend.”

“Yeah, I figured that, you tell Lay?”

“Yeah, she comin down Friday; we gon’ stay at my dads.”

“Right, I heard that.”

“I still got tha realtor look’n for a nice crib we can move into once you move up here.”

“That’s what’s up, so did Sash tell you that tha prom stuff was done?”

“Yeah, you know we had to get 2 made.”

“For what?”

“Her prom and mines.”

“Oh Shit, I forgot all about that; Nigga you crazy, I would have rocked that shit for both.”

“Yeah me too but you know how Lay is.”

“Just like Sash, so what colors y’all rock’n for yours?”

“Ivory and peach, I called and told him we need tha same measurements but instead of pink, we need peach. Well, I’ll hit you later, let me knock this homework out.”

“No doubt.”

CHAPTER 22

Kaí's Birthday Party, He Gets Shot!

I woke up feel'n good as Shit this morning; my dad said that him, Lay, and my mom were taking me to breakfast. Once I showered, I went into my closet to find tha perfect outfit for tha day. My party was tonight, damn I couldn't wait to see how many people were going to come to support me. I ended up put'n on my black Ralph Lauren sweat suit wit a white T and Air Ones. When I got downstairs, my dad tossed me his keys to tha 6 and said let's go. When I got to tha door and seen my dad's new 09 S600 sitt'n on dub dueces I looked at him and said, "You definitely snap wit this one Dad. You gon' be tha first dude in tha city wit this."

He looked at me smiling and said, "Nah not me, you."

I couldn't believe my ears so I asked, "What did you say?"

"You heard me."

"Just say it again Dad to make sure I heard you right."

"You heard me right, it's yours."

I hit tha alarm, when I opened it, "Damn! Y'all gon' make a nigga teary eyed."

Lay looked at me and said, "Happy Birthday Baby!" Then helped me put it on.

After we ate, we dropped my mom off home and my dad at his detail shop that he just opened.

"I'll see you tonight at tha party," I said while pull'n off.

"Aye Bugsy, you know ya peeps is having a party tonight in Wilmington."

"Yeah, that's why we gon' be in tha build'n stunt'n extra hard."

"I know all tha so called ballers will be out tonight in full force, Imma throw on my Louis Vuitton Shit."

"I heard that, Imma keep it basic. Prada button up, nothing major."

"Well, I'll be back 9:30."

"Cool, make sure you grab up some good green and a few "E" pills."

"I got you."

My phone started to ring, just as I got out tha shower.

"Yo."

"Hey, what's up Cuz."

"Just got out tha H20. What's tha deal?"

"Me and Sash on our way down."

"That's crazy I had to hear it from Sash that you push'n tha new S600 on 22's."

"My bag Cuz, I been ripp'n and runn'n all day."

"Wow, a nigga turn 18 and don't even know how to act. So that's how we gon' do it?"

"Naw Reek, stop that."

"I'm just play'n Cuz."

"I know but on tha real, we should be there in tha next 20 minutes."

"Well on that note, let me get dressed."

Lay walked in tha room and made me lose my breath. She looked like America's Next Top Model wit her brown and cream Elevee dress that accented every and I mean every curve wit her match'n stilettos. And to top it off, she had on her Ms. Jackson necklace and bracelet along wit diamond earrings and Carther frames.

"Kaí, Kaí..."

"Oh huh?"

"Did you hear what I asked you?"

"Lay, you had me in a trans."

"Boy shut up."

"Nah seriously, well, what did you ask?"

"Do you like my hair?"

She had it pressed so tha curliness was out for tha night. Anyway, there was a knock on tha door.

"Lay can you get that; it's probably Sash and Reek." After 15 minutes, I was dressed and on my way downstairs.

"My dad called, are you going to come to ya own party?"

"Yeah, I'm on my way now."

"Well, I'll be out front."

"Aye Dad."

"Yeah, what's it look'n like?"

"Just let me say this, if you don't hurry up you might not get into your own party."

"Here I come. We better hurry up my dad said or we might not get in."

"I like that Kaí," Sash said referring to my gear.

I had my brown Gucci blazer, blue Gucci jeans wit a tight fitted brown Gucci shirt and loafers wit my Gucci frames, DBD necklace and bracelet, and Marc Jacobs watch.

"Thank you," I said, "now let's get out of here."

"We gon' follow y'all." We went into tha garage and came out ready to roll.

Reek rolled down his window, "Damn, tha first nigga in tha city wit tha new S600 and sitt'n on dueces to top it off.

I smiled said, "Rockstar AR Track 1, Volume 15." All you heard was "Ya Boy Got Swag, Something ya Man ain't Neva had wit my Prada, Gucci, Louis Vuitton Bag. I Bet ya Man Can't Afford that, Baby I Got Swag."

"Damn Baby, I like this. Who this?"

"Oh it's my peeps. He bout to get signed to J. Records."

"That's what's up." When we pulled up at tha Chase it was J-peed and tha line was around tha corner. My dad was standing out front wit my uncle Pounds and his boys. I rollled down tha window.

"Yo!"

"No you didn't. Oh, you try'n to make me step my game."

"All tha way up."

"Kaí park over there," he said point'n to where they had parked at tha security moved tha cone so we could get in.

Once we were all out, Me and Reek walked back over wit 2 of tha baddest chicks on our side.

"Hey Kaí."

"What up Kaí."

"Happy Birthday Kaí."

"I like ya new whip Kaí."

"Can you get us in Kaí?" Was all I heard as I walked pass and spoke to tha ones that spoke to me.

"I see somebody has a fan club."

I looked at Lay and said, "Nah, I'm just good peeps. You know how that is."

When I reached my dad he let me know that my mom and her crew were already inside.

"Lay and Sash, ya moms is in there too wit ya Aunt Shonny and her crew."

"Oh, are they?"

I winked at Lay and said, "yup."

Pounds said, "Oh that's their daughter? I should have known; they look just alike."

We all went in, of course we didn't have to pay. We stopped to get some flicks from Shorty. All tha flicks were hot but tha one wit me and my dad. And Lay was right, my dad had on his Gucci Shit too but black wit his icy DBD chain and bracelet. Also, my dad had braids like Reek, I rocked my 360 waves.

As soon as I walked in tha showroom DJ Dougie Doug said, "Here is tha Birthday Boy!"

Everybody went crazy! It was so packed it didn't make sense. Everybody wanted to dance but I kindly let them know I was there wit my girl.

"Come on Lay, let's find my dad."

"There he go over there."

I turned to look, "I should have known."

We went over, "Dad."

"What up Kaí?"

"Is it a'ight if I drink?"

"It's ya birthday, do what you want." I went to tha bar and got a bottle of da best Shit which was that Ace of Spade.

"Put ya money away Lil Cuz, I got you." I turned around to find Bugsy and Slim stand'n there.

I grabbed tha bottle then said, "Good look'n Cuz." Then made my way to tha dance floor.

A bottle in a half later I was drunk; my dad came over, took tha bottle from me then said, "Looks like you're ready to leave."

I asked him if he was ready and he said that he wanted to stay until it was over. I was drunk but I knew how to control it; I wasn't fall'n down or none of that dumb stuff other people be doing when they get drunk.

My dad said OK then him and my mom left, I was ready to go. When they put on my song "Never" by Jahem, me and Kaí slow danced to that. I knew it was going to be a love making night.

At 2:30, everybody started to leave; when we got outside tha parking lot was packed. It was like tha party went from inside to outside. We walked passed this one group of dudes who I could tell just came for tha let out. By tha way they were dressed in "all black" if I didn't know any better, I would have thought they were to scope out who to rob. I had already took Kaí's jewels off when we were in tha party. They weren't gon' catch my baby slip'n.

"Ain't that tha nigga who's party it was?" Another dude pulled out tha flyer he had in his pocket.

"Yeah, that's him."

I didn't like tha sound of that so I tried to walk a little faster, especially since Reek and Jerz had already left. I just wanted to get to tha car before something went down. I knew it was about to go down when I heard one of them say, Birdman you ready? They started walk'n in our direction.

"Yo Kaí."

"What's up?" Kaí said turn'n around.

"Let me holla at you for a second."

Kaí said, "I don't know you."

"Yeah but you will," dude said pull'n out his rachet.

"I knew that something was up wit them niggaz, I just knew it," Kaí thought to himself.

"Nigga you know what it is; run ya pockets!"

"I ain't got Shit Motha Fucka!"

"Oh, so you a Bad Ass," he said walk'n closer wit his gun pointed directly at Kaí's chest.

I said, "Empty ya pockets," Kaí was about to say something but I cut him off, "Baby just do what they say."

"Yeah, your best bet is to listen to ya Bitch!"

I knew as soon as "BITCH" left his mouth it was about to go down. Kaí caught him square in his mouth causin him to fall and drop his gun. Tha other dudes pulled out, all you heard was "BONG! BONG! BONG!" Everybody started scream'n and runnin for cover; tha 4 dudes ran also. I see Kaí on tha ground wit blood runnin from his body.

I dropped down and screamed, "Somebody call an ambulance please!" I held his head, "Baby please stay wit me."

My Aunt Shonny ran over, "Oh Shit," she pulled out her phone, she was so hyper, "Jerz, Jerz Kaí just got shot!!!" She was cry'n try'n to explain then she put her phone down.

Tha ambulance had pulled up tha same time Jerz did. I had my hands on his chest and stomach where he'd been shot to stop tha blood. Tha paramedics told me to move but I was in shock. My mom had to move me that's when I lost it.

"Noooo! Nooooo! My Baby! They Shot My Baby!!"

They had to call tha helivac because he lost so much blood. After they had him in tha helivac tha paramedics let us know that they were taking him to Christiana Hospital. I didn't know where that was so Jerz told me to get in tha car wit him and told my mom to follow.

But before he left he yelled to no one particular, "Did anybody know them niggaz that did this!" When nobody answered he said, "I got 100 g's for anybody who knows anything!" Then he got in and pulled off.

I couldn't stop cry'n even while I told him what happened.

"I do know that one of tha guy's name is Birdman. I heard one of them call him when we first came out."

By tha time we got to tha hospital, Kai's mom and a few other people were there. We all stood around until tha doctor came out. By then tha wait'n room was packed.

"First, let me say that you're," he said point'n to me, "the only reason that he's still alive. Had it not been for you applying pressure to those holes, he would have definitely died. But for the next 72 hours, it's touch and go."

I was tha first to speak, "Can I please go in and see my baby?"

"Yes, you can, he's not in a coma."

"Is he..."

"No, he's very much alive, he's just weak."

Me, Jerz, and his mom went in, as soon as I seen all those tubes in him I lost it. I vowed to never cry after my dad was murdered but here I am like Rick Ross cry'n over another man that I love dearly.

"I sat in tha car and watched as Birdman and his crew stood around wait'n for Kai to come out. They were gon' come out and Birdman was supposed to rob him then kidnap him."

"Here he comes Bugsy," Slim said. I hung up my phone and watched thru tha tinted windows.

"Damn Bugsy, don't look like Kai gon' give it up peacefully."

Next thing I knew, 3 shots rang out and my little cuz was on tha ground. At first I thought he was just lay'n there so he wouldn't get hit until I heard Lay scream.

"Oh Shit! Bugsy they shot him!" We stayed to see what tha damage was. I knew it wasn't good when they had to fly him to tha hospital.

"Oh Shit Slim, you hear that? My unc got a 100 stacks."

"We can't do that Bugsy cause them niggaz will tell in a New York minute."

"Yeah, you probably right."

"Ain't no probably Nigga! Shit we might just have to pop they top for safety measures."

"I'm feel'n you on that one Slim."

"Well, say no more."

CHAPTER 23
Who Did This?

A week had passed and Kaí's condition was upgraded from critical to serious and he was moved to a more comfortable one-person room; because of all of tha visitors he was gett'n his room was filled wit balloons, cards, and flowers. I walked in to find some broad and her friends in his room. I never jump to any conclusions so I put tha flowers on tha windowsill and tied tha balloons to tha bed.

"Hey Sexy," he said, "what's up?"

I looked at him then said, "I don't know, you tell me."

"Let me introduce you to my cousin Jada. Jada this is my girl Lay."

"Oh, I need to thank you for saving my cousins life."

My aunt said, "If it wasn't for you that he wouldn't be here."

"I don't need to be thanked; I did what any girlfriend would have done."

"I heard that," she said wit a smile, "well Kaí, I'll be back later this week, I have to be at work in a little."

"Ok Cuz."

"Do you need me to bring you anything?"

"Nah, I'm cool." I watched as they walked out.

"Well Ok, which one of her friends like you?" That caught me totally off guard.

"What makes you think one of her friends like me?"

"Boy please, a woman knows when another woman likes her man."

"That's not important, all you need to know is that I don't like any of them. I only have eyes for you."

"I hear you." He tried to sit up, I could see tha pain in his face.

"Baby just lay there, that's what this is for," I said using tha pad to raise tha bed in a sitt'n position, "just use this and you'll be fine."

"Lay, I need to find out who did this."

"No, you need to get better and let ya dad and Reek find out who did this to you; for that 100g's somebody gonna talk, you can believe that."

"What 100g's?"

"That's what ya dad is offering for anybody wit information on who did this."

"Well, if it wasn't for you I wouldn't be here. My mom says I owe you my life."

"Nah, you just owe me ya love."

"You already got that and even if we don't be together forever, you'll always be my best friend."

"You promise."

"I promise."

"Tha doctors say you should be able to leave in another week or two at tha latest."

"I can't wait, I need some real food. Not to mention, I lost a few pounds."

"A few? If you lose any more we won't be able to see you," Reek said walk'n in wit Sash, Shy, and my aunt Rose.

"Kai!" Shy said runnin to give me a hug.

"UGH!"

"Shy be careful," my aunt said also giving me a hug, "when ya dad told me what happened I just prayed that you would be alright. I told y'all those clubs."

"Mom, it was his birthday party, how would that look him not showing up for his own party?"

"He has a point there Aunty."

"I'm mad about my T-shirt."

"Boy please," Sash said, "just be happy you're alive."

"I am but that was a $150 Gucci T-shirt."

"So do tha police know who did it?" We all looked at one another but then we had to remember who was talk'n.

"Nah Mom, they don't have any leads or suspects as of yet but I'm sure that they will."

"They better hope tha police find them before I do," Reek said.

"Boy what you mumblin about?"

"Nuffin Mom."

My aunt started going into tha Bible; if tha nurse hadn't come in to change my bandages she would have definitely started preach'n to us like she always does, and truth be told, she be right. But you know how it is when you don't want to hear tha truth, especially when it hits home. But none tha less, that's my aunt and I love her to death.

"Kai why did somebody shoot you? Were they mad you had a birthday party?"

"I don't think I want any more birthday parties Mommy." We all started laugh'n.

"Baby that wasn't why they shot him."

"Then why did they?"

One thing about Shy, she would not stop until she got tha answer she wanted. My aunt gave us that look that said help me out.

"They shot me because they wanted my money."

"Oh well, why didn't you just say they were try'n to rob you." I started laugh'n so hard my stomach started bleeding.

I didn't notice until Lay said, "Call tha nurse! Hurry up!"

When she came in and took a look she let me know that 2 of my staples had come open and that I had to take it easy. She handed me 2 Percocet's; within 10 minutes I was drowsy. Next thing I knew, I was sleep.

CHAPTER 24
Hit tha Lights

"Hit tha lights."

We cruised down tha block real slow. I was in position wit my AK out tha window. As soon as we came up on them I let my AK ring. TAT, TAT, TAT, TAT, TAT, TAT, TAT, TAT They both hit tha ground, I had to be sure they were dead. I jumped out wit my mask on and put a few more rounds in them causing their bodies to jerk. What life that was left was now gone. I hopped back in tha car and we spcd off, now headed to Birdman's house. When we pulled up tha block was isolated and all tha lights in tha house were out. I knew he wasn't home because it was only 8 o'clock. But no sooner as we parked he was pull'n up, I pulled out my phone.

"Yo what's tha deal Birdman?"

"You My Nigga."

"What's tha verdict on da boy we hit?"

"He gon' make it."

"Where you at?"

"I just pulled up to tha crib."

"Me and Slim gon' come by I got a job for you, if you interested."

"Fo' sho my nigga."

"A'ight give me 15 minutes."

We sat in tha car and bust it up for 20 minutes then walked to his crib. Before he could knock on tha door, Flocco was pull'n it open. This was even better, now we had tha last 2 ducks in tha same place. We couldn't have asked for anything better. We walked in Birdman was in tha kitchen cook'n up some coke.

"Damn Nigga, smell like burn'n that Shit up!"

"Nah, it was something on tha burner."

I looked at Slim, within seconds we both pulled out and let off 3 shots apiece to make sure they were dead. We put one in each of their dome out tha stove off and walked out as if nuffin ever happened.

It had been a month since Kai had gotten shot and still we had no clue. There had been 4 murders in Salem since then but nobody had no idea who was behind them and tha papers weren't say'n a word. We had opened up our shop last month and business was already doing extremely well. I was so proud that we had took illegal money and made it legal. I was on my last appointment when Reek had walked in.

"Hello Sexy."

"Hey you," I shot back.

"Is that your last client?"

"Yes, why?"

"I wanted to take you out to dinner."

"I'll be done in about a half."

"A'ight, I'll just wait," he said flop'n down on tha sofa, "y'all look'n at this?"

"Not really."

"So is it OK if I turn?"

"Yeah, as long as it's not sports."

"Come on Babe, you know my Lakers are play'n tha Suns."

"Actually I didn't."

"Well now you do."

"Oh you being smart."

"No not at all."

"I didn't think so, go head."

I turned just in time to see Kobe knock'n down a 3-pointer to tie tha game right before halftime. As soon as Sash was done tha 3rd quarter was about to start. I looked at her.

"Don't even think about it." Her client started laugh'n.

"Girl I go through tha same thing wit my husband. Here you go Sash, keep tha change."

"Ok thanks Ms. Emily."

"No problem, you keep me tight so I have to do tha same."

Ms. Emily was about 50 but still looked to be in her 30's. Her daughter had brought her in when we first opened and she's been here every week since then faithfully.

"So, where do you want to get something to eat from?"

"I don't know, it doesn't matter."

"Did Kai come up this weekend?"

"Nah, he has therapy on Saturaday so he said he'll be up afterwards."

"How is he doing?"

"A lot better, he's finally start'n to gain his weight back."

"I told Lay she might as well move to Wilmington as much as she's been down there. Only time I see her is in school or at tha shop when she decides to come. But I feel her because I would be tha same way if it was me."

"Well, that's nice to hear."

When we arrived at Ruby Tuesdays, Slim and Bugsy were there wit some broads. I just nodded and kept it moving. I don't know I just got this funny feel'n they had something to do wit it because one of tha boys that got earthed in Salem name was Birdman and I doubt that it was a coincidence. I'm gonna find out and so help me if I find out they had anything to do wit it. Imma pop they top! Brother or not!

CHAPTER 25

Our Prom was tha Bomb

Tha prom was less than two weeks away and my baby had gotten his weight back. I think him gett'n shot gave him this I don't give a Fuck Attitude. He told his dad he was in tha game and to my surprise he said that he already knew. But what he didn't know was they had tha same supplier, gett'n it for tha same number.

Kaí said his dad asked him how much money he had and what he was grab'n; when he told him, his dad was not surprised but impressed that he had so much in so little time. Kaí had even started smoking weed, I kinda liked this bad boy side in him, it turned me on.

I had a 10 o'clock appointment who was late. She finally showed up, my 11 o'clock was already in tha chair.

"Lay, I'm sorry I'm late, I had ran into a little problem wit my baby's father. He left me to be wit some trick, now he thinks I'm suppose to jump when he comes runnin back. He had me hostage, begg'n for me to forgive him and I probably will; I just want him to beg and suffer for a while. Let him see how that Shit feels and even after I do I'm gon' treat him like Shit for a while."

"Bitch you crazy," one of tha other girls said.

"That Shit ain't cool," one of tha barbers said.

"Joe shut up, he get'n what he deserves."

"See that's tha problem wit you females, a man makes a mistake and when he realizes it, you want him to jump thru hoops to get back. That Shit gon' backfire on you, then you gon' be tha one hurt in tha end."

"I was tha one hurt in tha beginning."

"So that makes it right to do tha same thing? Two wrongs don't make it right, you have to just forgive and move on. Notice I didn't say forget cause you never forget."

"Damn Nigga, you sound like Dr. Phil Raheem," another barber said.

This was usually how it went in our shop every day. It was always good topics and conversations.

"Oh Shit! Turn that up!" There was a breaking news story.

"Two men were found dead in a parked car outside the Elks Home in Camden Heights. Police believe it was robbery related or as they say a drug deal gone bad. The names of the victims have not been released and will not until family is notified. If you have any information about this please call the number at the bottom of the screen. For KA TV this is Pete Adams reporting live at Camden Heights."

"See that's tha type of Shit right there I be talk'n bout. It ain't even safe to go to tha clubs no more."

"Lay you know that, look at what happened to Kai a few months back. Niggaz is so thirsty they'll do anything for a drink of water."

Tha next few days flew by; it was prom night. We decided to rent tha new Bentley Limo. Once I was dressed I felt like a princess and Reek was my prince. Tha outfits we got made were tha bomb; we definitely didn't have to worry about anybody having on tha same stuff since ours were handmade. We walked in Lay's house and my mom Ms. Jean and Jerz all had their cameras.

"Y'all look very nice," my mom said all smiles.

My dress was all red wit black stitch'n wit a pair of Jimmy Choo stilettos while Reek had on a black tux wit a red shirt and red Gucci loafers. I couldn't front, when Lay and Kai came downstairs they looked fantastic. Lay had on her all pink and ivory dress wit tha shoes to match while Kai had a ivory suit wit a pink shirt and pink Versace loafers wit ivory stitch'n. We took a lot of pictures then got into our Limo headed to tha prom. When we pulled up we weren't tha only ones step'n out a Limo but we were tha only ones to get out a Bentley Limo. I felt like a celebrity tha way everybody were snap'n their cameras. They even had a red carpet set up wit a picture booth so you could get ya picture taken before you went inside. Everybody kept tell'n us how good we looked. Most of tha females got their hair done at our shop, either by us or someone that worked there; and same for tha guys. We were considering opening another shop.

Tha prom was tha bomb, I was happy that Lay got to enjoy herself after all that she has been through tha past few months. Me and Reek were voted prom King and Queen. All in all, our prom was tha bomb!

CHAPTER 26

Tha Contract wit Mr. Malony

"Yo niggaz ain't ain't gon' play wit my paper. If you owe then pay, if not, get ya top popped. That's how it's going down."

"What's up wit ya man Bugsy? Did he ever pay that stack he borrowed?"

"Twist that was so long ago, I forgot about that Shit."

"Well, I didn't. After doing 5 years that's all I did was think about niggaz that owe. Do ya cousin Slim still run wit that Nut Ass dude?"

"Yeah, they still hang'n tough."

"You know what he did? Hit me plus he gave me an extra nickel."

"Oh, so he up?"

"He doing his thing."

"Let's slide over there so I can get some loot from his Punk Ass."

"Come on, let's go." When we pulled up, him and Slim was sitt'n on tha green box.

"Slim, that ya cousin Raheem?"

"Where?"

"Right there park'n."

"Oh yeah."

As soon as they walked up I said, "Oh Shit! Look Bugsy, they don' let this nigga out of tha cage."

"What up Slim?"

"Bugsy what it be like?"

"Same Shit, different year."

"Here Slim," Raheem said hand'n me two $100 bills.

"That was good look'n tha other day."

"Ain't bout nuffin, we fam."

"Well a nigga fresh out, hit me." I gave him one of tha 100's Heem just hit me wit.

Bugsy said, "I'm tapped right now." I could tell Twist didn't like that answer because he grabbed Bugsy's pocket.

Bugsy smacked his hand away then said, "Nigga you must have been down too long, don't ever grab my pockets again."

Twist started laugh'n, "Oh, you got heart now huh?"

"You must got me mixed up, I always had heart. I said I'm tapped and that all it is plus; I don't owe you nuffin."

"Heem you better let ya boy know alots changed in 5 years."

"Yeah you right, you don't owe me nuffin but know this...from here on out if you want to sell anything out here it's gonna cost you."

"Twist what I look like pay'n you to hustle on my block."

Bugsy started laugh'n out of nowhere. Twist punched him in tha face. I started to pull out but Heem stopped me.

"You don't got Shit to do wit it Cuz." I already knew what was about to happen, Bugsy got up and said, "Damn, you will'n to die on ya first day out."

"Oh so you threat'n me?"

Bugsy pulled out his .40 cal and said, "I don't make treats." And let his cal ring, 5 shots hit Twist dead in tha chest.

This time Heem was about to react.

"Like you told me Cuz, you ain't got Shit to do wit it."

And just to make sure Heem would be wear'n Twist on a shirt, Bugsy stood over top of him and said, "I'll see you in Hell!" And fired a single shot in his head.

Before we stepped I said, "I hope you don't sell us out Cuz." By tha look on his face I knew he would take it to his grave wit him.

I drove by just in time to see some dude punch Bugs in tha face. When Slim went to reach, tha other dude stopped him. When I got closer, I realized it was Raheem. As soon as I seen Bugs pull his .40 cal I knew what was about to happen, I kept driving.

"BONG, BONG, BONG, BONG, BONG!"

I didn't even bother to look in my rearview then I heard another shot. I just drove to Old Man Smitty's to meet Kaí so we could pick up our shipment from Sanchez. When I pulled up I honked tha horn to let Kaí know I was outside. He came out wit tha duffle bag. After we finished meet'n wit Sanchez, we had another meet'n wit Scott tha Realtor. He had a few nice 3-bedroom houses, he wanted us to look at. When it was all said and done, we ended up wit a 3-bedroom, 2.5 BA Ranch style wit a 2-car garage, full wall out basement, and tha price we bought it for was a steal. We had my unc do all tha paperwork. It was on tha outskirts of Jersey in a quiet part of town. We didn't want to be in tha city so this spot was low key for us.

"Reek, I think I'm going to ask Lay to move in wit me if that's a'ight wit you."

"Why wouldn't it be? We both paid for this house plus I was going to ask Sash tha same thing. So of course it's a'ight wit me. If Lay moves in we'll all be one big happy family."

Reek was about to say something when my phone rang. I looked at tha caller ID then said, "Hold that thought…hey, I was just talk'n about you."

"Oh you were."

"Yup."

"Wit who?"

"Reek."

"Well, what could you possibly be talk'n to Reek about me?"

"Well, we just purchased a beautiful 3-bedroom house, I wanted to know if you would be interested in moving in wit me."

"I don't know, I havc to think about that one."

"Well, just take ya time."

"Boy stop play'n, you know I want to move in wit you. Ain't gon' be known trick'n in that crib."

"Yeah right, even if you didn't move in, you would probably be there so much it would be just like you lived there."

"I know huh. So can I do tha interior decorating?"

"Sure, but you gon' have to share that duty wit Sash cause I know she gon' say yeah to Reek when he ask."

"On some real Kaí, we were gon' get a crib together. We thought it was time to let our moms get some privacy."

"I heard that. Damn, so you basically say'n let them get their freak on in peace."

"Boy ain't nobody say'n that but you."

"Well, I might have said it but you was think'n it."

"Hold on Kaí, that's Sash." (CLICK)

"Hello."

"Girl, I got some good and some bad news which one you want first?"

Tha bad news I already knew what she was going to say but I played along.

"Well, I'm afraid I'm not going to be able to move in wit you."

"Why not?"

"There's where tha good news comes in. Tyreek asked me to move in wit him." Lay kept me on hold too long so I hung up. She can hit me when she done talk'n to Sash.

"Damn Kai done hung up, now I got to hear his mouth about not click'n over to say I would call him back."

"Oh, so you diss'n me for Reek? Wow, I see how it is now but it's cool cause Kai asked me tha same thing."

"Husy why you play'n. I was gett'n ready to say that since Kai was going to be living there that I would probably see you all tha time anyway."

"So, we need to go see this house so we can see exactly how we gon' do tha Damn thing."

"I let Reek know that he and Kai could do whatever they wanted to do wit tha basement. He said as long as I didn't make it all girly."

"Sash he must don't know we gon' do tha same thing." We was gon' to do our Shit Gucci downstairs and Prada up since we already got tha stuff ordered.

"We just need to call and give them tha address, it won't be here for another week anyway."

"Well, I'm about to meet Reek so I can go see this house."

"Ok, call me when you get done. I'm gett'n ready to call Kai back so he can cuss me out for leaving him on hold."

"My bag, you should have said something. I would have called you back."

"Girl please, he'll be a'ight. That's his problem, he is spoiled but Imma break him out of that."

"Lay you crazy. Well talk to you later."

As soon as I hung up I called Kai, to my surprise, he didn't even trip. He didn't even say anything about it.

"Lay where you at?"

"I'm at home. Why?"

"Well, be ready in 15 minutes. Imma scoop you so you can see tha house."

Within 20 minutes he was pull'n up. By tha time we got to tha house, Sash and Reek were comin out.

"I can't even believe that nigga Twist try to play me like that. If Raheem wasn't ya peeps, I would have put some hot shit in his ass too. I hope he don't run his mouth."

"Nah, you ain't even got to worry about that. Raheem knows tha rules to tha game. So what's tha deal wit Mandy? She ain't got nuffin else lined up for us yet?"

"I'm glad you said that, I was suppose to have lunch wit her today but I had to do a few things so I let her know that I would make it up by taking her to dinner tonight."

"Well, did you decide what you gon' do about y'all living arrangements?"

"Yeah, I was gon' let her know tonight. I figured since she only a half hour away, I would just move in wit her so that she wouldn't have to sell that house since she just bought it.”

“I feel you plus you don’t want her to be where all ya chicks at anyway.”

“I ain’t worried about that, Imma probably start cutt’n them off anyway.”

“Damn, let me find out Mandy got you whipped like mashed potatoes.”

“Nah, it ain’t like that, I’m just ready to settle down. Maybe have a kid or 2. Shit tha way I’m living tomorrow ain’t promised and somebody got to carry on tha legacy when I’m gone.”

“It’s crazy you said that, I was think’n tha same thing.”

“Oh, you try’n to settle down?”

“Hell Nah, I’m talk’n bout tha kid part. I just got to pick who I want to have my seed, Raylonda or Shonda.”

“Why not both?”

“Cause, I only want one.”

“I hear you on that. So what’s up wit Reek and Kaí, you still policing them?”

“Yeah but them dudes a lot smarter then I gave them credit for.”

“Why you say that?”

“First, they got Sasha and Layla out tha game then I don’t even think they touch’n that Shit because tha way I been on them for tha past 2 months I haven’t seen ‘em touch nuffin. So I need to figure out who they got moving that Shit for them.”

“Maybe they ain’t been doing nuffin tha last 2 months; you know we still in recession.”

“I know, I even thought about that too but I know a few people who has still been cop’n off them and they said that either Reek or Kaí been bring’n it to them; no one else. But for tha life of me I just can't figure it out but when I do, we gon' cash in like we hit tha Jackpot."

"Hello."

"What up Reek."

'I can't call it Spit. What's good on ya end?"

"Down to tha last 3."

"By tha time you done it will be in tha same spot. But after this time, we gon' switch it up just in case somebody has been watch'n."

"I feel you on that."

We had Spit doing all tha runs; we were charging him 20g's a brick and he was loving it. We just didn't want to take tha chance of somebody try'n to get tha drop on us. We also let Sanchez know we wanted to switch locations which he had no problem wit. Once we found another storage place, ery thing was set in motion. Sanchez had started hitt'n us wit so much coke it wasn't even funny. Tha crazy thing is, tha more we got, tha faster it went. We had branched out to Virginia, North and South Carolina, Atlanta, and DC. So to say we were movin major Shit would be an understatement.

"Aye Reek, I think it's time that we invest some money into a few legal things."

"How about if we holla at Mr. Malony? You know his construction business is in a major debt."

"How is that wit all tha jobs they do?"

"My dad said he was talk'n to him and that's what he said."

Reek's dad had been work'n for Malony and Son's for Damn near 15 years, If not more.

"Well, call ya dad and see if he could set up a meet'n wit him." Once it was done I looked at my watch.

"Damn Reek, we only got 30 minutes. We might as well leave now."

When we pulled up to tha site where we had to meet Mr. Malony my dad was stand'n out front; he greeted us when we walked up.

"Come on, Bill is inside wait'n on you."

As soon as we stepped inside tha trailer he stood to greet us.

"Good afternoon Gentlemen."

"Same to you Mr. Malony."

"Please call me Bill. What can I do you 2 young men?"

"Well, let's get straight to tha point, I understand that you are in danger of losing your business that you worked so hard for." He gave my dad a look that said why did you tell anybody.

My dad said point blank, "Bill, now is not tha time to let your pride stop you from gett'n help that you badly need."

"Well, I doubt that they can help me."

"If you don't mind me ask'n, how much are you in debt Mr. Malony?"

"1.5 Million." Tha look on our faces must have said it all.

"I use to have a serious gambling problem a few years back. I had lost a lot of money behind that. I actually had lost money that I didn't even have at tha time so that's how I got into debt."

"What about all tha big contracts you do?"

"That's where tha money went into, pay'n back tha loans then I had to pay my workers."

"So, when does this loan have to be paid off?"

"By tha end of next month."

"So this is what we will do. We give you tha 1.5 million that you need but we want to be part owners. We also know a lot of people who need things done that will be very profitable for tha 3 of us. If you agree wit that, we'll have our lawyer draw up a contract that you can have your lawyer go over. But tha clause is that if by any chance you fall back into your gambling ways, you surrender your part of tha business to us; making us sole owners. Now, if you have no problem wit that then we'll get tha paperwork started and have it over by later this afternoon."

"On that note, I'll be wait'n for tha contract."

When we were back in tha car I said, "This calls for a nice Dutch."

We had our lawyers draw up tha paperwork and take it over. Once Mr. Malony signed it, we then gave him tha 1.5 million he needed to pay back his loan to whoever he had owned.

CHAPTER 27
I'm Movin Out

Tha furniture had finally come and I was glad, my mom was starting to trip. I think it was because I was moving out on my own and she was going to miss me not being around. I asked Jerz if he could introduce her to one of his friends that were single. He let me know that he would look into it and get back wit me. I wanted my mom to be happy and now that I was leaving home tha only thing that would bring happiness into her life would be a man.

"Lay, I hope that Jerz has a friend; I want her to be happy like Ms. Jean."

"I feel you cause ever since my mom started dating Jerz 9 months ago, she's been nuffin but happy. It makes me feel good knowing I had something to do wit it. So I do feel you on that. On tha real, that's probably tha only reason she ain't trip out when I told her I was moving out. All she said was am I sure that's what I want to do."

"Lucky you, I had to go through a thousand questions. She almost looked like she wanted to cry."

"Well Sash, you are her only child so what do you expect."

"I guess you're right but I'm ready to move out. She needs to get over it."

I couldn't believe how good tha house looked once ery thing was in play, even Kai and Reek were impressed. Now all we needed to do was move our belongings in.

CHAPTER 28
We're Being Followed

We were on our way to meet Spit when I noticed we were being followed. Just to make sure, I swung a few corners and sure enough so did tha van.

"Don't turn around but this van has been following us."

Kai adjusted his mirror so that he could see what was going on. He punched in a few numbers on tha radio and just like magic tha secret compartments slid open. He wasted no time grabbing tha 2 pistols that were in there.

"When you get to tha light bust a left then a right and park. Imma walk into one of my friend's house and slide out tha back door. I just need to be on point in case I got to body whoever it is." As soon as he parked I hopped out, slid in, and right back out tha back door.

I twerked Reek, "Yo, they still there?"

"Yeah."

"A'ight, I got them." When I came thru tha cut they never even seen me coming. I ran down on them and put my .40 dead in his face.

"Who are you and why tha Hell are you following us!"

His boy tried to reach but I let him know if he did his boy would be dead so he put his hands up. By this time, Reek was on his side wit his desert right at his head.

"I believe he asked you a question?"

"We don't know his name, tha guy gave us 10 stacks and said don't lose you."

"I'm not buying that! Now let's try it one more time! Who sent you?!"

I asked cocking my pistol Bugsy and Slim.

I looked at Reek, "OK now tha game has changed; I'm going to give you another 5 stacks. Bring them back to this address. All you need to do is tell them you seen us go in there wit a few duffle bags."

I saw that look in their eyes, greed they weren't going to do nothing but try and make as much as they could. So without warning, I fired a single shot into his head. Once I did, Reek did tha same then we walked back into tha cut. We hoped that nobody seen us. We walked back out tha front door, nobody had even come outside. When we got back into tha car I put tha pistols back where they were. Then Reek pulled off slowly so that we didn't cause any unwanted attention.

"So, what do you think about that?"

"Before I answer that, why did you put his brains in his lap." I explained it to him and he totally understood.

"Well, I think it's time that Slim and Bugsy learn a lesson. I looked him dead in tha eyes to show my seriousness.

"Reek you want to hear something crazy? Tha boy Slim came to me on da low a few weeks ago try'n to cop some work. He said that he wanted to hit his young boys wit some work. I didn't know what his motive was so I told him that I was still on hold. I also told Spit not to sell them niggaz nuffin. I don't care if they wanted 10 bricks. I'm try'n to spare his life but this nigga keeps crossing that line of trust." Kaí just looked at me.

"Don't he know Trust is Ery Thing?" he asked hold'n up his left hand to expose his tattoo.

"I don't want to put Aunt Rose through all that pain and grief."

"Neither do I but he's giving me no other option. He's at his second strike, one more and he's out. Imma pop his top, I promise.

When I picked up tha paper tha first thing that caught my attention was **TWO MEN FOUND DEAD SHOT IN THE HEAD NO MOTIVES, NO CLUES, NO SUSPECTS.** I read on, they didn't have tha names but I was pretty sure that it was Joe and Dave. Tha block they were found on was a known drug block.

"What were they doing on that block when they were suppose to be following Reek and Kai? Could they have...Nah, they don't even know they were being followed." Slim walked in wit tha paper.

"Oh, so you saw tha front page."

"Yeah, I'm gon' just fall back on my brother."

"Well, Mandy called, said she got something real sweet for us and tha pay off should be lovely."

"I'm bout to go holla at her so she can fill me in. You want to roll?"

"Nah, I'm getting ready to go holla at Shonda to see if we can go half on a baby."

"I hear you playa playa."

"Just hit me when you find out ery thing."

I pulled up, honked tha horn 2 times and waited for Jean to come out. We have been seeing one another for almost 9 months and I still hadn't made an attempt to sleep wit her. I was just letting her know that I could care less about that and show her that I liked her for her. Tonight I was taking her to somewhere special. When she had finally come out, she was look'n amazing. I got out to open tha door for her; I grabbed tha bag and put it in tha trunk.

"Damn, I said to bring an overnight bag, not a weekend bag."

"Oh be quiet, you know how I am."

"Always packing extra, you never know."

"Well, smart ass if you know then there shouldn't be nothing to say."

"Yeah, I guess you right."

"Ain't I always?"

"Do I really need to answer that."

"Nah."

"I didn't think so," changing tha topic I said, "you look beautiful."

"Why so do you."

I pulled up to tha loading dock, got out and opened tha door for her; still tha perfect gentleman.

"Wonder how long this is going to last?"

"Oh so you're say'n when I stop opening doors I won't be tha perfect gentleman anymore."

"Not at all."

I grabbed our bags out of tha trunk. I had rented a yacht for tha night. We boarded and were greeted by tha Captain.

"Good evening Sir, Madam, I'll be holding you down for tha night. Let me show you to your cabin." When we got to tha cabin it was amazing, it was like a mini apartment.

"Please make ya self at home. When dinner is ready somebody will be back to get you," he walked out.

"I hope this will be a night you'll always remember."

"He said that when we when we went to tha Bahamas. I remember

alright, I remember nothing happened."

Once we put our stuff away, there was a knock on tha door. When I opened it there was a man stand'n there in a tux.

"Dinner is ready, if you would please follow me."

He showed us to tha dining area which was beautiful. There was one table in tha middle of tha room wit a dozen roses in tha mood. As soon as we were seated, they begun to bring tha food out. Then I heard tha soft sounds of I believe it was Luther Vandross *"If Only for One Night."* As we ate and enjoyed tha live band, I knew that this man who sat in front of me had totally made me fall in love. He stood up, took my hand, and led me to tha upper deck. When I looked out I was in awe for 2 reasons. One, I had no idea that we were moving; I thought we were going to stay docked. And two, now tha moonlight which glowed on tha ocean was breathtaking. I looked at him in his eyes then told him that I loved him and I hadn't felt this way about a man since Layla's father was alive. He took his hands and wiped tha tears from my eyes. He returned my stare then let me know he loved me also. I was overwhelmed, I wasn't even expecting that.

"Let's go," he said leading back to tha cabin.

When he opened tha door and I saw all those rose petals on tha bed and floor I just knew it was on.

"Is it alright if I take a shower?"

"I was hoping you asked that."

I went into tha bathroom to find a nice bubble bath wit rose petals on top and Musiq Soul Child playing on tha radio. I took my clothes off and sat down in tha tub; boy did it feel good. I was drifting off to sleep when a soft tap on tha door brought me back to life.

"Come in," I said. Jerz came in wit a box.

"When you're done put this on. I'm going to go take a shower."

"There's enough room in here for you."

"Nah, that's just you." As soon as he said that I knew my kitty cat wouldn't be purring tonight.

As soon as he left I got out, opened up tha box to find a red panty and bra set wit matching rob from Victoria Secrets. I laid across tha bed, I must of dozed off because I never heard Jerz come in. I just felt his hands rubbing my body.

"Umm that feels good." I didn't let myself get to aroused because this is what he always does.

"I got her right where I want her. She's most likely thinking that I'm only gon' rub her back and lick on her. Not tonight, she was in for tha night of her life." I removed her robe along wit her panties and bra.

"Here we go again," I thought to myself.

As he rubbed and licked my back he surprised me when he ran his tongue on my butt causing me to moan. Then he turned me over and started kissing and caressing my nipples wit his tongue. He worked his way down to my love nest. As soon as he touched that little man in tha boat I felt my body jerk. He just kept going, by tha time he was done I had climaxed 4 times. Shit Lay's dad couldn't even make me do that. I wanted him inside of me but I waited until he was ready. I tried to go down on him but he stopped me saying, "Tonight is all about you." When he inserted his man inside of me I had to scream from tha pain. But within a few strokes tha pain was replaced wit pleasure. When we were done I was exhausted. Jerz definitely gave me a workout and I loved every minute of it. This was tha best sex I've ever had. I thought Lay's dad was tha truth. He had nothing on Jerz, if I didn't know it before, I really knew it now; I was in love. It was definitely worth tha 9 month wait.

Tha next morning, I woke him up by returning tha favor and judging by his facial movements, I hadn't lost it in that area either. I let him do his thing then licked him clean. Jumped on that horse and rode into tha sunset.

CHAPTER 29
Tha Kidnapping

"BALTIMORE POLICE! EVERYBODY DOWN!!!"

"Slim put tha restraints on them. Is there anybody else in tha house?"

"No," tha female said.

We tore tha house up until we were sure. We had it all, for some reason I had a feeling there was more. I went into tha pantry that was in tha kitchen even though Slim had checked. I double check hitting tha walls wit my hand.

"Bingo!" I said.

I used tha end of my shotty to bust a hole in tha fake wall and sure enough there were 3 large duffle bags. I took them out, when I looked in tha first one I almost pissed myself. I didn't need to look in tha other 2.

"Grab that, let's go!" We had it all now.

"Y'all have a nice day," I said as we walked out.

We exchanged cars and headed back home wit our earnings. By tha time we made it home, it was 3 in tha morning. I looked in tha other two bags and couldn't believe my eyes.

"Slim, get tha money machines."

It was damn near 9 in tha morning when we were done counting all that money. I felt sorry for those dudes, they were going to have a lot of explaining to do.

"You know I might just retire from ery thing."

"Why would they have this much money in their house?"

"I don't know and I don't care, it's our doe now." Now we came away wit close to 5 million.

"Hold on Slim, I remember a few months back a bank down there got hit for close to 7 mill. They got tha guy but tha money was never recovered."

We both looked at each other and said, "Oh Shit that explains why it was wrapped tha way it was."

"So we give Mandy 1 million and keep 2 apiece."

"That will work for me."

"Yeah, Imma fall back for a minute. Enjoy some of this money."

"I'm gon' invest some of mines."

"In what?"

"I don't know Bugs; I'll figure that out in a few days."

"Ain't no way Imma go broke off this or get caught up in some dumb shit mess'n wit this nigga."

"Slim, Slim."

"Yo."

"Damn Nigga."

"My fault, I was try'n to think about what kind of business to start up."

"Well, let me get on tha road before she start blowing my phone up." Sure enough, by tha time I got halfway home she was calling.

"Hello."

"Damn you forgot where home is."

"Nah Babe, I'm like 10, no 5 minutes away."

"Well, what's wrong, did ery thing go as planned?"

"Yeah."

"Well why you sound down?"

"I'm tired as hell," I said pulling up.

"I see you out front," she said look'n through tha blinds then opening tha door. I got out wit tha bags. I walked in tha door and handed her tha bag that was hers.

"It's a million in there but you can count it if you want to."

"Did you just say a million?"

"Yeah, that's what I said."

"Well, if I got that what was ya take?"

"2"

"Damn Baby."

"I know, that's tha same thing I said. I'm done wit this robbing Shit, I'm gon' use this to start me a business; go legit. I just need to decide what kind of business. You know I was think'n about buying houses and fixing them up and leasing them to Section 8."

"That's a good ideal."

"Or starting my own taxi service or both; I don't know."

"Baby I'm glad that you gon' do something positive cause this was tha last time for me; even though y'all was doing tha work. I just don't want in on it, I have more than enough money to last tha rest of my life. Plus, I'm about to be a mother in 6 more months." She kept talk'n but I was blown away.

"Mandy did you say you was gon' be a mother in 6 months?"

"Yes I did."

"Is it mines?"

"Nigga don't disrespect me, you tha only one I been sleep'n wit for tha past 2 ½ years. I use to be a stripper but I'm no whore!"

"I wasn't try'n to say that."

"Well then, what was you try'n to say?"

"I just asked a question that any man would have asked. If you got offended, I'm sorry," I pulled her to me, "you know I love you and that I wanted a baby. So you 3 months?"

"Yeah, I went to tha doctors yesterday for my yearly checkup and he told me I was 12 weeks."

I couldn't believe it, I was gon' be a daddy. I was definitely done wit tha game. I'm gon' get me a new phone today. I'll see Bugsy when I see him.

I was gett'n tha last of my stuff when my mom came in wit her overnight bag and a big smile.

"Umm, Umm, I see somebody finally got their selves some last night."

"Lay what are you talk'n bout?"

"Come on, I felt and had tha same look when I first got some from Kaí. So you finally gave in huh Mom?"

"Lay it was him, I been ready to give him some."

"So tha apple doesn't fall too far from tha tree, I see. Mom I haven't seen you this happy since Daddy was alive."

"I haven't been, no one can ever take his place but Lay I can't lie, he does make me happy and I love him a lot."

"Well from what Kaí tells me, his dad never spent this much time wit one woman. So he knows you got him." That made her smile.

"Well, he told me that he loved me last nite."

"So you really moving out?"

"Yeah, I think it's about time. Plus, you and Jerz gon' need ya privacy now that y'all have elevated to tha next level," I said giving her a wink.

"Yeah, you probably right."

"But don't think that you're not going to see me."

"Oh child please, I know I'll see you."

"So when do you plan on giving him a key?"

"Not any time soon, he has to earn that."

"Well after that stellar performance you said he put on last night I would have thought he did."

"Lay you are a mess."

"Well, let me get on my way before Kai start calling."

"Where's he at?"

"He went to tha shop to cut some hair today. Before I forget, you know they just got that big contract wit MBNA."

"Oh yeah that's good, I'm glad to see that their making some money wit that construction company."

"Well, call me later, I need to get a little rest before my hot date tonight."

I pulled up to tha shop, it was J peed like it usually is but for some reason it was standing room only. Tha 4th of July had already passed so it wasn't a holiday coming up. When I walked in like 4 of my clients were in there. I had to look at my appointment book to make sure I didn't have any appointments that I might have forgotten about. And like I thought, I didn't.

"Hey Lay," Iesha said, "I know I don't have an appointment til next week but can you squeeze me in? You know tha Playas Ball is tonight."

"Oh Shit, it is? I don't know why I thought it was next Friday. That must be where my mom and Jerz are going. Well, it's a good thing I already got my outfit."

"Who you telling," Sash said.

"I'm going to need you to touch me up."

"A'ight cause I need you to flat iron mines."

Kaí smiled then said, "That's how you doin it." He loved when I wore my hair like that.

"I ain't fool'n wit you, you didn't even remind me."

"Awe Babe, I thought you knew it's only tha biggest event of tha year that brings 'em out," Reek said.

"Nigga if it wasn't for ya dad you forgot too." Tha whole shop started laugh'n.

"Damn Reek, that's how you feel? It's cool."

"Go head wit ya tender ass feelings," Annett another stylist said.

"Y'all gon' leave my baby alone," I said stick'n up for him.

"Nah Lay, I got them; might not be today but I got them."

By tha time we had finished up it was close to 8 o'clock and tha 4 of us still had to get our hair done. While Kaí was cutting Reek's and I was curling Sash up. When we were finished we all admired what tha other did.

"Kaí, I like that look on you. I didn't think you were gon' look right wit ya beard dyed black."

"I know, me either. My dad told me to try it out."

"I'm feel'n it though."

I was glad we had 2 bathrooms, we knocked 4 birds out wit 2 stones. Of course, me and Kaí had to get it in while we were in tha shower. After everybody was dressed, we headed out. I didn't know why they called this tha Playas Ball; it should have just been called tha Fashion Ball. Tha first person I saw when I walked in was my mom look'n sharp wit this all-red Christian Dior dress and match'n shoes.

"Now who are you here wit?" I asked as if I didn't know already.

For tha past 3 months, she had been dating one of Jerz peoples. I didn't know, I had just found out after I moved out and came to tha house unannounced. Let's just say, she was in tha middle of something. I was glad that she had finally gotten herself a man, friend, or whatever you want to call him; but he's good people.

"What up Sash, Reek, Kaí, and Lay."

"What up Speedy."

"Y'all look'n nice."

"Thank you," we all said at tha same time.

Lay and Kaí had on Gucci and we had on Prada.

"Lay, did you see ya mom yet?"

"No, we just got here."

"Oh well, here she comes now." I turned around to see her and Jerz walk'n arm and arm. My mom was glowing wit happiness.

"Why y'all always try'n to be like us?" Kaí asked because they had on some Gucci.

"Don't forget who turned you on to Gucci. I had you rock'n Gucci before you could even pronounce it let alone spell it."

He was right.

"Anyway, y'all look nice."

Tha party was live, they had a surprise performance by Rick Ross. At tha end of tha night, I was feel'n good. I guess I had one Apple Martini too many and by tha looks of it so did Lay. On tha way home, I let Reek know that I had a good time. We were suppose to be going to Jamaica in 2 weeks, I could not wait.

It had been 3 weeks since our big hit and I hadn't heard from or seen Slim. I was a little worried, I didn't know Mandy's number or where they lived so I had no way of finding out if he was okay. I called all tha local hospitals but he wasn't in any of them. Unless, he used a fake name which I know sometimes he did, but I didn't know tha names he used. I was down to 700 grand; I had lost big in Atlantic City last week. I had a sweet plan to get a nice piece of money but I needed Slim to pull it off. If I didn't hear from him in tha next few days I would just do it by myself. A whole week had elapsed and still no Slim. I had called up my mans from Philly that I did a few jobs wit awhile back and he was wit it. Once tha plan was set in motion there was no turning back.

"Remember this is my peeps so do not hurt either of them."

"I got you."

We pulled tha ski mask down on our face and hit tha door hard. As soon as I heard tha screams I knew they were both downstairs. We quickly tied them up and put tha tape around their mouths. I felt bad for doing this but hey I had no choice. We took them outside and put them into tha van. Once we had gotten them to tha safe house I gave Cheeze tha phone. We had rehearsed it so much he had it down. As soon as they picked up, he went right into it.

"Listen and listen close, it would behoove you to not hang up. Especially if you want to see ya mom and sister alive again. Before you start wit tha who is this, who hired you Bullshit. Let me tell you how much it's gon' cost you. I need 5 million dollars and you have one week. And just to let you know, this isn't a game." I snatched tha tape off both of their mouths causing them to scream. Then I put it back on, never once taking off their blindfolds.

"Hello"

I listened to this guy talk. At first, I just thought it was somebody play'n on tha phone until I heard my mom and Shy scream. But who would have done some Shit like this and for 5 million? Now we were gett'n money but we didn't have 5 million just laying around. Tha thought of someone hurting my mom or sister brought tears to my eyes. When I hung up, Sash looked at me.

"Babe, is ery thing alright, what's tha matter?"

I yelled out for Kaí who came runnin along wit Lay. When they got in our room I didn't say anything, I just wiped my tears.

"What's wrong Cuz? Talk to me." I still didn't say anything, I picked up my phone and dialed.

As soon as my uncle picked up I said, "Uncle Jerz can you talk?"

"Yeah, what's up."

"I just got a call from who, I don't know but they have my mom and Shy. And they said I have a week to come up wit 5 million dollars." I saw tha look on everybody's face.

"Well, did they say anything else?"

"No."

"Well do you have tha money?"

"No, I only have about 2," Kaí said.

"I got about tha same."

"And we have tha rest," Lay and Sash said, "so there you go."

"Don't worry about gett'n back, I got you. Where are you now?"

"I'm at tha crib."

"I'll be by in 30 minutes."

"I'll be here."

When I hung up I felt like this was all my fault. But who could or would do something like this? Kaí looked at me wit tears in his eyes.

"Don't worry Cuz we gon' get them back and we gon' kill whoever is responsible for this. Is that all tha money y'all have?"

"Yeah but we just re-up yesterday so we got tha work to bounce back."

"But if they could do it once, what's stopping them from doing it again? We gotta move her out in tha burbs even if she doesn't want to go."

45 minutes later, my dad was at tha door.

"So have they called yet?"

"Nah." Just as he was about to say something Reek's phone started to ring which he immediately picked up.

"Hello!" he yelled into tha receiver.

"Damn Nigga why tha harsh tone?"

"Look I don't have time to play these games, I have ya money. Tha next questions are when and where?"

"Well, I'll call you back wit all of that info." Then tha line went dead. My uncle put his finger up then went outside. When he came back, he was carrying a black duffle bag. He sat it on tha table then opened it up. When I saw all that money I was wondering what was goin on.

"This 2.5 million, so y'all just put tha other half up. If I had more I would have used that but this is all I have left." We all looked at him.

"What?" We all thought.

Kaí said, "Dad you broke?" He started laugh'n.

"Hell no, this counterfeit money that I have for situations like this; I thought I had more. I'll turn you on to my peeps so if this ever should happen again it won't cost you too much." I had to look at tha money again.

"It doesn't even look fake."

"It's not suppose to, if it did it wouldn't be any point. Don't get me wrong, it will spend but if you get caught that's a Federal charge." He started laugh'n.

"What's so funny?" Lay asked.

"I can't believe y'all thought I was broke."

"Well you did come in here wit this duffle bag of money talk'n bout that's all you had left. So what were we suppose to think Dad?"

"I don't know but not that." Tha sound of Reek's phone brought us back to tha reason we were all stand'n here in tha first place.

"Hello." All he said was Southeast corner of Cherry Hill Mall. Once we have tha money I will call you to let you know where ya peeps is at."

"How can I trust that once I give you tha money you'll let my family go?"

"Like I said Southeast corner." Then line went dead.

"What did he say?" I repeated to them what he told me.

"I do know that it's more than one person." Sash asked how did I know.

"Because he said when we have tha money. We've wasted enough time, let's go! Sash, Lay y'all stay here." When we arrived at tha mall it was packed like always on a Saturday. We went where he said to be and within 5 minutes my phone was ring'n.

"Hello."

"See tha trash can to your left, put tha doe inside and go around by tha Food Court entrance."

Kaí got out, put tha 2 bags inside and got back in. I drove to tha Food

Court. It took 15 minutes but they finally called.

"It was nice doing business wit you. I see that you love ya mother and sister."

"Dearly."

"Tha blue van, that's where you'll find them."

Before he hung up I let him know that if I ever found out who he was I was gon' kill him and whoever was involved in it wit him. We opened tha van wit our guns drawn to find my mom and sister tied up wit blindfolds and duct tape. They were happy to see us.

"Did they hurt y'all?"

"No, they treated us very well." I hugged my mom and let her know I was sorry.

She looked me dead in my eyes then said, "Baby I don't blame you; you have no control over what another person does. But you do have control over your actions and decisions you make. That goes for all 3 of you."

"So are you ready to take him up on his offer to move out of tha city?"

"I'm not moving anywhere because if they want to find you they will."

"Well, so then I guess we'll just have to upgrade your house."

Tha ride back to my moms was a silent one. As soon as we pulled up and I saw tha door.

"Nah Mom, go get you and Shy some things, y'all gon' stay at our house until we get this door fixed." Shy was happy about that.

"Is Sash and Lay going to be there?"

"Yup, they sure are."

"OK cause you know them my girls." Even my mom had to laugh on that.

We got back to tha house Lay and Sash had tha crib smelling like some good soul food. I was starving like a bear in tha woods.

"Umm you ladies got it smelling real good in here. I hope you got enough for 2 more."

"Um excuse me but I think you forgot me."

"Well, I'm glad we cooked enough food for you guys," Sash said pointing to me and Kai.

"Imagine that," Kai said.

We all sat down and enjoyed dinner.

CHAPTER 30
Tyreek Learns who Kidnapped His Peeps

"Didn't I tell you that we would come up."

"Yeah, that was a hell of a score. How did you know that they would give tha money up?"

"Because it was my cousin, brother, and uncle well."

"If you don't mind me ask'n, who was tha women and little girl?"

"My mom and sister."

"Damn Nigga you a cold-hearted nigga. Why do that to ya moms?"

"Nigga did I hurt them?"

"Nah."

"A'ight then it was all about tha money."

"I feel you but Damn."

"Here go ya cut 2 million just like I told you. Don't spend it all in one place."

I had to manage this money right; I can't afford to mess this up. I think I need to get back into tha game to make sure this money expands. I need to find me a connect. I don't know what's up wit Slim; I haven't heard from him in about a month. Now I'm beginning to think that he's avoiding me but why would he be doing that. I need to find out where he lives at to see what's really good.

"Slim."

"What up Babe?"

"Did you go check on ya business license."

"Yeah, they told me I can pick it up tomorrow which is good cause tha

2 cars I bought will be ready in tha morning. So, Imma probably drive one until I can get 2 drivers."

"Baby, I'm so proud of you, you really doing something legit."

"I have to, I want to be around to see my seed grow up and be able to secure a future for us."

Tha next few months shit was start'n to look up. I was even proud of myself, I had finally came up off of a legit hustle. I should have been doing this Shit. I wonder what Bugsy is up to, I haven't heard from him in a few months since we did tha hit in B-More. I'll call him in a few days just to check up on him.

"Hello."

"What up Reek?"

"I can't call it, what's good wit you Lil Nigga?"

"Awe you know, try'n to make it do what it do. I was about to shoot to Philly to do a little shop'n; you try'n to roll?"

"Nah do you, I got some Shit to handle. Hit me when you get back."

"A'ight."

I jumped in my whip, headed to Philly. When I got up there I found a spot right in front of tha Net." As I was put'n money in tha meter somebody came up on me from behind.

"Give that Shit up Nigga!" I started to pull my pistol out.

"Hold on Nigga." I turned around to find my cousin Cheeze stand'n there.

"Damn Cuz, you was about to get ya top popped."

"I saw you reach'n that's why I said hold on."

"Damn when you get home?"

"I been home for a few months now."

"So you work'n?" He gave me that look that said come on.

"I see you look'n good." And he was, bait on his neck, nice leather, I knew he was up to his old tricks.

"So you still put'n in work huh?"

"Nah, I gave that shit up. I can't even front, I did one sting when I first came home but it was enough to make me fall all tha way back."

"Damn it you must of had a serious hit."

As a matter of fact, I did tha hit in Camden."

"Yeah?"

"Yeah, I helped some nigga kidnap his mom and sis."

Oh Shit!" I thought to myself I know he can't be talk'n bout Reek's mom and sister, Imma ask him.

"By any chance was tha nigga named Bugsy?"

"Yeah, you know him?"

"I use to cop off him awhile back."

"How you know it was Bugsy?"

"On some real shit, I be deal'n wit his brother."

"I ain't know, I don't want no Shit."

"Nah, Imma make sure you not involved."

"That's what's up. So what's good wit you? Looks like you eat'n," he said pointing to my 645CI I had sitt'n on dub dueces. I had upgraded from my Park Ave.

"Well, take my number, hit me up. I got to meet this shorty for lunch. A Cheeze, how much did y'all get?"

"5 million."

"Damn you sitt'n lovely."

"Yeah, I got 2 out of it."

"A'ight then Cuz." As soon as I stepped off I called Reek.

"What up Lil Homey?"

"I'm on my way back, I need to get at you ASAP."

"Well, just hit me when you get close."

"Damn, how was I gon' tell my mans that his own brother is tha one that had his mom and sis kidnapped."

I made sure I called soon as I got close. He let me know that he was at Old Man Smitty's house. When I had pulled up, there were a few friends working around so I got out and asked them why they were working. Then Reek came out followed by Kaí. Once they finished conduct'n business they walked over. I was leaning on my car.

"So what's so important?"

"Remember when ya mom and sister were held for ransom?"

"Yeah why?" he asked looking at me wit concern on his face.

"Did they get 5 million?"

"Yeah, how you know?"

"You not going to believe this when I tell you." Now instead of a calm tone, it was replaced wit an eager to know tone."

"Well, while I was up South Street I ran into my cousin; he had just gotten out of jail a few months back. We bust it up, I wanted to know if he was still into robbing niggaz. He let me know that he wasn't but for him to had just come home he was too fly. Then he told me that when he first came home, he did a hit that netted him 2 million. Now that's a lot of bread from a hit; then he said it was a hit from my way. So I asked who it was, that's when he told me that he had helped some boy kidnap a lady and little girl." As I looked at Reek his face now held tha look of murder.

"Actually, he said it was tha boy's mother and sister."

"Hold up, hold up Kai said, "did you just say mother..."

Before he could finish I said Yes and I asked if by any chance tha boy name was Bugsy? They both waited for tha answer they already knew.

Kai couldn't take it, "So what did he say, Spit?" I just nodded my head. Reek pulled out his phone, pushed a button then put tha phone to his ear.

"Where you at? You up this end? A'ight, come to Smitty's...10 minutes, a'ight." He put his phone back in tha case. Once I seen Jerz pull up I knew it was going down. I didn't know if I should stay or not so I said, "Before I go, I just want to say that if my cousin has to go then I want to be tha one to pull tha trigger."

"Imma keep it 100, ya peeps was fresh out; he didn't know who's people he was kidnapping. Even though I don't feel anyone doing that to anybody's but I say that to say he gets a pass."

"Did I miss something?" my uncle asked.

"Yeah you did." I filled him in.

He looked at me,

"You know what has to be done."

"I know so check it, this is what we gon' do..."

After we finished talk'n we all knew tha game plan. I was just happy that I wouldn't have to kill my cousin and I wasn't going to tell him that he could possibly have that fake money.

I was so hurt to know that my brother would stoop so low to do that to his own mother and sister. Whether or not he hurt them was besides tha point; that's a line you definitely do not cross. And not only did Bugsy cross it, it was his 3rd and final strike. He had put my mom into a dangerous situation and robbed us for 2.5 mill which we had gotten back in tha last few months. I told my uncle not to mention this is my mom; I didn't want her to know we were going to be tha ones to cause her grief and heartache.

Over tha next few days I had talked to Sanchez, he let me know that my unc had told him about Bugsy. He said that he could have somebody take care of it but I let him know that I wanted to be tha one to handle it. I didn't want anyone not even Kaí or my unc to have his blood on their hands. And that was tha truth, I needed to be tha one which he totally understood. When it first took place, he had offered to front us some work but we were cool. We had just scored tha day before. Bugsy did that nut ass shit so we had more than enough work to get back but that let me know if we ever needed him he would be there for us. Tha next day, my mind was racing wit a thousand and one thoughts. I was suppose to be at tha shop at 11 a.m., I had a few heads to cut but I wasn't in tha mood to cut no hair. Sash called my phone.

"Hey Baby."

"Hey."

"You a'ight? You been distant since you talk to Spit."

"It's a lot of Shit that's been going on that has my head all messed up."

"Well you know you have 3 clients here wait'n on you."

"Is Kaí there? Ask him if he can take care of them for me."

"Kaí's not here either and he has 4 people wait'n. Lay called, and he said he was on his way. I hope you two are not in any trouble."

"Nah, well I'm on my way."

30 minutes later, I pulled up in front of tha shop. I reached in my back seat, grabbed my CD player, breezed through it and found what I was look'n for then headed into tha shop. I went straight to my station not speak'n to anybody; I went straight to work. Kai must have been on tha same page because he walked in wit his Walkman on and went straight to his station. I could see tha whole shop watch'n us but they did not understand what either of us were goin thru. We knew that what we had to do would hurt but our plan was set; we wasn't turning back. When I finished my last head I looked at Kai who gave me a nod and nuffin else needed to be said. I let Plies take my mind off of what we were about to do in a few hours. I just imagined how Reek had to be feel'n.

I caught Lay peep'n over at me a few times but I was in my bag so I just stayed in my zone like A.I. I was on my last head when Reek looked over at me. I just nodded then turned up tha volume on my CD player "My Dog went to Court they Gave Him 15 Young Little Nigga. He was 16 Don't They Know What all that Time Mean..." As soon as I finished my last head my phone started ring'n.

When I answered all they said was, "Let's go!"

I grabbed my jacket and headed for tha door. As soon as Kai walked out my phone rang,

"Yo come on, it's time!"

I grabbed my jacket, headed towards tha door, and Sash stepped in front of me. She didn't say anything, she just gave me a kiss and walked off.

"Lay I don't know what's going on but it's very serious."

"I know, I could tell by tha way they were acting."

"Yeah, Reeks been quiet since yesterday."

"Girl, Kaí has been tha same way. I knew something was wrong when he didn't want none of this good pussy I was try'n to give him."

"Lay you crazy as Shit."

"I'm dead serious, I just hope both of them a'ight because between me and you they ain't been tha same since Ms. Barbara and Shy were kidnapped. Well, I'm done for tha evening, I'm on my way home to start dinner."

"A'ight, I'll see you when you get home. Can you stop by tha LQ and grab me a pint of Grey Goose and 6 pack of coolers."

"Yeah." I went to reach in my purse but she said that she had it.

"Well, I'll be home in tha next hour."

"A'ight."

CHAPTER 31
A Meeting wit tha Kidnapper

I had called Bugsy and told him that I wanted him to handle some business wit me. I knew that he wouldn't expect anything. He told me he would be ready when I got there. I pulled up, honked tha horn and Bugsy came out. I could see tha bulge in his shirt from his pistol.

"You don't need that," I said point'n to his pistol.

"Oh my fault." He ran back into tha house then came back out. Once he was in tha car, I pulled off.

"Where we going Unc?"

"To this warehouse, I want to introduce you to some people who can make us very very rich."

"You know I'm down wit that." My phone started to ring.

"Hello."

"Oh what's up."

"Yeah, I'm in route now. Are you already there? I'll be pull'n up in tha next 15 minutes." (CLICK)

"Was that ya peeps?"

"Nah, that was Kaí." He had this crazy look on his face when I mentioned his name.

"It's time that y'all put this bickering to tha side and think about tha bigger picture which is all this money we bout to accumulate. Now if you don't want to get this money then I can take you back home."

"Nah, I'm good as long as them niggaz play they part we cool."

I looked over at him then said, "Nah, as long as you play ya part."

He probably wanted to say I don't need y'all. Damn, I loved my nephew but he had done tha unthinkable and if he really knew tha game he would have known not to ever involve family. He let greed blind his vision. When we pulled up Kaí, Reek, and Spits cars were already there. We got out and walked in, they were all seated at tha table; we joined them.

I started by say'n, "Tha reason for this meet'n is to instow family values."

"He ain't family!" Bugsy stated point'n at Spit. Spit looked him dead in tha face.

"Nigga I'm probably more family than ya Faggot Ass!" Now Bugsy was up on his feet.

"Nigga what did you just say?" Spit sat his pistol on tha table.

"You heard what I said."

Damn, my unc made me take my shit back in tha house; I sat back down.

"He's a Dead Ass Nigga."

"Enough of that Shit. Spit, do you love ya mother?"

"Of course."

"How about you Kaí?"

"Yeah."

"Reek?"

"Wit all my heart Unc."

"And you Bugsy."

"Of course, that's a dumb question." I couldn't hold back; I raised my voice.

"You're a Fucken Lair! If you loved your mother you would never have done what you done to her!!!"

Damn, what is he talk'n bout, I was wondering if he was talk'n to me. I stop wondering when he took out his pistol and pointed it at me.

"Hold up Unc, what are you talk'n bout?" Reek punched me in tha face.

"Nigga you know what he talk'n bout Mother Fucker! It was you that kidnap Mommy and Shy!" He couldn't even lie, his face said it all. I pulled out my .40 cal, smacked him in tha head.

"Nigga, I'll put ya brains all over this floor. How could you do something like that to your own mother!"

"She did not get hurt, did she?"

"It doesn't matter, that's ya mom!"

"Well, I knew if I gripped up those 2 Bitches that y'all wouldn't pay that much for them."

Without think'n Kaí pulled out his pistol "BONG!" He shot Bugsy in tha leg.

"AAAAAAAAAHH! What did you do that for!"

"You lucky I only hit you in tha leg. Don't ever disrespect my girl."

"Fuck you and ya girl."

"Oh that's ya word."

Kaí pointed his desert at his other leg, before my unc could stop him, "BONG, BONG!" He hit Bugsy in tha other leg twice.

"AAAAAAAAAHH!

AAAAAAAAAHH SHIT!"

"Now what was that gangsta shit you was talk'n?"

"Sikaí if you pull that trigger one more time Imma put my foot in ya Ass." Reek started laugh'n.

I pointed my pistol at him, "Oh that Shit funny."

"Nigga I know you ain't gon' pop me so put that shit down."

I lowered my gun because he was right, I wasn't gon' shoot him. I looked at my dad, all he said was "WHAT?"

"How much of that money do you have left?"

"I don't know."

"Listen, I know that we said we was going to kill him..." At tha sound of that, Bugsy started throwing up all over himself.

"But instead of killing you, were going to put you away for life. Right now as we speak, tha Feds are tearing ya house up. So those pistols wit tha bodies are going to get you life, maybe even tha death penalty. And tha money you got from us is all fake so you'll be gett'n charged wit that as well. Actually I'm lying, I had tha guns taken out but all that fake money that you have in there, they'll find it." We all looked at my dad like he was crazy.

"I know y'all are probably wondering why I called or had somebody call tha Feds, I would rather see him in jail and not dead. If you disagree wit me feel free to kill him." We all looked at one another then at Bugsy.

I laid there think'n that I would rather go to jail then die. Plus, Imma put tha Feds on all of them faggots

So I thought, *"Damn, if we let this nigga live he gon' turn on us without hesitation."* We all pulled our triggers.

BONG! BONG! BONG! BONG! BONG! BONG! BONG! BONG! BONG! Tha 3 of us, me, Spit, and Kaí let off 3 shots a piece.

"I need to ask, why did y'all shoot him?"

"Dad if we would have let him live we would all be caught up wit Fed cases by tha time he was done."

"Damn, I was think'n tha same thing."

Reek added, "Me too."

"Well, I lied about tha Feds being at his spot. I knew if I said that y'all would do exactly what y'all did. Next question, do you want him to disappear for good or should I let my sister bury her oldest son?"

"Unc on some real, I think it would be best if we let her bury him because if he just disappears she won't be able to sleep a lot of nights."

"Yeah, you right nephew. So where do we put him?"

"On his doorstep."

CHAPTER 32

Death B-4 Dishonor

That night when I got home I didn't feel any remorse or sadness. When I walked thru tha front door all I could smell was fried chicken and boy was I starving. My unc said he would take care of Bugsy's body. Kaí came in 15 or 20 minutes after me, he went upstairs and got straight in tha shower. I had done tha same thing when I had first came in. By tha time he came down I was already at tha table get'n my grub on while Lay and Sash were in tha living room watching that show The Unit.

"Ya plate is on tha stove."

He put it in tha microwave then sat down to eat. We looked at each other and smiled knowing exactly what tha other was think'n. When we finished we sat down to join tha girls. Kaí pulled out his Dutch that he already had rolled up. Since he was tha only one that smoked, he didn't even bother to pass it.

"Let me get a pull of that Cuz." Lay and Sash both looked at me.

"What? I ain't allowed to smoke."

Lay said, "Did you hear us say anything?"

"You didn't have to, ya faces said it all."

"Let me get a shot of that," Kaí said point'n to tha bottle of Bombay that sat next to Lay on tha floor.

"Well, I see that both of you are in a better mood than you have been in since you left earlier."

Sash looked at me and said, "If you don't mind me ask'n, what was tha matter?"

"It's better you don't know so that way if shit ever hits tha fan you really won't know what's going down."

"You ain't got to say no more, as long as you not keep'n no secrets."

"Nah Baby, as bad as I want to tell you I think it's best that I don't." Kaí just gave Lay that look that said don't ask.

Tha next morning, I got a call from my mom she said she needed me to go to tha morgue wit her to identify my brothers body. To my surprise, she didn't sound shaken up at all.

After I picked my mom up, we headed to tha Medical Examiner Office to identify Bugsy's body he led us to a small room. When we got inside there was a body on a silver table wit a sheet over it. He pulled tha sheet back and sure enough Bugsy was laying there. My mom showed no emotion and nodded her head yes. When we got back to tha car my mom looked at me then said, "I'm not mad at you." I looked at her.

"Why would you be?"

"I know that you killed your brother."

"Why do you think I did it?"

"Because your brother was tha one who took us hostage." That statement completely caught me off guard.

"If he could do something like that then he had no love for me or Shy. I know he was my child but to be so cruel and do that to me tha woman who gave birth to him. I'm probably tha reason he's lying on that stretcher; I wished that on my own child," my mom started crying, "what kind of person am I to wish death on her own flesh and blood?"

"Mom, it's not your fault. How did you know that it was Bugsy that had kidnapped you?"

"I heard them talk'n on tha phone and a mother knows her child's voice. I just kept it to myself; I didn't want to tell you or Jerz because I know you live by tha code Death B-4 Dishonor and Rashawn dishonored tha trust code." Tha rest of tha ride was a silent one.

"Tha only reason I did that is because no matter what reason, he did what he did. At tha end of tha day, you are his mother. I don't care what kind of life I was living I would never hurt you."

"Baby I know you won't. Now I don't agree wit tha lifestyle you live but you're doing what you believe is tha best thing for you. I just wish you as well as Kaí and my brother would just leave that business alone."

"Mom, I'm not going to be hustling forever. I just need to make sure that I'm financially secure and that you and Shy are as well."

"Baby, we are more than alright, believe me. I haven't been working all my life for nothing." All I could do was smile.

"I had funds set up for tha 3 of you in case something ever should happen to me."

"First of all, you ain't going nowhere anytime soon and if something did happen I would raise Shy to be tha young lady you wanted her to be."

"Tyreek, I know that you would, I just want you to be careful," she said as we pulled up to tha house to be met by my uncle and Sikaí; they both hugged my mom.

She looked at both of them and said, "I already know and it's partly my fault." Then walked into tha house, they both looked at me for answers.

"She told me that she knew it was Bugsy who kidnapped her and that she knew we were tha ones who had killed him. She also said that she wished he would die for doing that to her and Shy."

"Why didn't she tell us?"

"She didn't want us to do what we did. I let her know that he had crossed one too many lines."

Over tha next few years, ery thing was lovely. Slim had gotten out tha game, his taxi and real estate business were doing well. Mandy was due to have her baby in 3 months. My mom had finally moved out of tha city. My little sister was always over tha house wit Sash and Lay. My Uncle Jerz was still doing his thing and he and Lay's mom was still going strong. Sash and Lay had opened another shop called Style By Us. Not to mention, they both were expecting. I think they planned it that way but it was all good. As for me and Kaí, we were doing it big in tha construction world. Mr. Malony had started back gambling so we took over and renamed tha business to T & S Construction. Sanchez was still tha man, he would come by for holiday dinners. Oh and Spit, he was tha man he had Jersey on lock in a choke hold ever since we became silent partners.

Just always remember that Trust is Ery thing, without it you have Nuffin!!!

ABOUT THE AUTHOR

My name is Jerz Toston, I reside in Wilmington, Delaware. First, thanks to my fans for your continued support. This is my 5th book titled Trust is Ery Thing. My other four books are titled Compromised, Street Dreamz: Ery Thing Ain't What It Seems, Who Can U Trust? and Betrayal & Deceit are available now on all on-line bookstores. Also, you can call my publisher directly at 877.782.5550 x100 and them shipped to ya door.

Writing books is my passion and I'll continue to give you page turners. Just call me Ya Fav Author.

YA FAV AUTHOR

COMPROMISED

STREET DREAMZ:
ERY THING AIN'T
WHAT IT SEEEMS

WHO CAN YOU TRUST?

BETRAYAL & DECEIT